"I know I'm gruff
time..."

Gabe cleared his throa[...] but...I have to say... Well, the little pink [...] grown on me."

Once he had spoken the first words, it seemed as if Gabe must spit them all out before he came to his senses. "They steal my time, they invade my study, they run down my hallways, and yet I went crazy thinking about Debbie being hurt. And still, I know the minute she can, Debbie will be right back out on that swing fixing to break the other arm." He looked up at Avery as though she were a puzzle to solve. "How do you do it?"

Explain parenthood to a bachelor cowboy? She could gather every word in Texas and still not have enough. "You just...do."

Gabe was trying so hard not to care.

He was failing at it, and in a way that stole her heart no matter what she deemed best for her or the girls.

* * *

Lone Star Cowboy League: Boys Ranch
Bighearted ranchers in small-town Texas

The Rancher's Texas Match by Brenda Minton
October 2016

The Ranger's Texas Proposal by Jessica Keller
November 2016

The Nanny's Texas Christmas by Lee Tobin McClain
December 2016

The Cowboy's Texas Family by Margaret Daley
January 2017

The Doctor's Texas Baby by Deb Kastner
February 2017

The Rancher's Texas Twins by Allie Pleiter
March 2017

Allie Pleiter, an award-winning author and RITA® Award finalist, writes both fiction and nonfiction. Her passion for knitting shows up in many of her books and all over her life. Entirely too fond of French macarons and lemon meringue pie, Allie spends her days writing books and avoiding housework. Allie grew up in Connecticut, holds a BS in speech from Northwestern University and lives near Chicago, Illinois.

Books by Allie Pleiter

Love Inspired

Lone Star Cowboy League: Boys Ranch

The Rancher's Texas Twins

Lone Star Cowboy League

A Ranger for the Holidays

Blue Thorn Ranch

The Texas Rancher's Return
Coming Home to Texas
The Texan's Second Chance

Gordon Falls

Falling for the Fireman
The Fireman's Homecoming
The Firefighter's Match
A Heart to Heal
Saved by the Fireman
Small-Town Fireman

Visit the Author Profile page
at Harlequin.com for more titles.

The Rancher's Texas Twins

Allie Pleiter

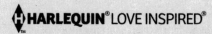

HARLEQUIN® LOVE INSPIRED®

Special thanks and acknowledgment are given
to Allie Pleiter for her contribution to the
Lone Star Cowboy League: Boys Ranch miniseries.

Recycling programs
for this product may
not exist in your area.

LOVE INSPIRED BOOKS

ISBN-13: 978-0-373-62260-3

The Rancher's Texas Twins

Copyright © 2017 by Harlequin Books S.A.

www.Harlequin.com

Printed in U.S.A.

Rejoice before Him—His name is the Lord.
A father to the fatherless...is God in His holy
dwelling. God sets the lonely in families,
He leads out the prisoners with singing.
—*Psalms* 68:4–6

For Kelly
A mom with grace and humor

Chapter One

Gabriel Everett had one job.

Well, two actually. One was standing in front of him, and the other was nowhere to be found. Spring in Haven, Texas, was shaping up to be one giant mess after another.

"So you'll consider it?" he said to the young woman sitting on the Haven Boardinghouse front porch. More like standing, for the pair of little girls at her feet hadn't let poor Avery Culpepper sit still for very long as he tried to hold a serious conversation. "You'll stay on just a couple more weeks until the celebration?" Gabe wasn't much for pleading, but she'd talked of heading back home and there was a lot at stake here. He had no intention of being the failing link in the long chain of events that led to the future success of the Lone Star Cowboy League Boys Ranch.

"Well," said Avery, handing a marker to one of her girls, "there's a reason I didn't respond to Darcy Hill's attempts to reach me. I didn't really want any part of this to begin with. And now, I have to say this isn't turning out well." One of the little girls began bickering with the other over the red marker. "I can't exactly put my life in Tennessee on hold while you all…look out!"

The box of markers tumbled off the table, covering Gabe's left boot in a cascade of colors. One of the girls lunged after the spill and careened into Gabe's shin. Was it Debbie at the table, so Dinah was clinging to his leg? Or the other way around? He couldn't keep the four-year-old twins straight—did Debbie have the darker hair or did Dinah? Then again, did it really matter which pair of hands was now smearing marker on his jeans?

"Oh, Dinah, look what you've done." Avery fished in her pocket and pulled out a lint-covered tissue as Debbie began to chatter an explanation—or an excuse. Gabe waved off the suspicious tissue and instead began wiping at the purple streak with his own handkerchief. His housekeeper, Marlene Frank, would have fun trying to get that stain out.

Avery already sported three similar stains of her own. He'd met this young mother only a handful of times since Darcy had convinced her to come to Haven, but already it stumped him how the poor woman made it through the day with her sanity intact. Kids mostly annoyed him—how did she stand that whining hour after hour? A single mom with twin four-year-olds—that was the very definition of *outnumbered* in his book.

Appeal to her practical side, maybe, he thought. "I find it hard to believe you don't want to know what your grandfather's will has in store for you. Could be an explanation. Or an apology for the way he wasn't there for you. Or maybe he's left you something significant, something you could really use."

She blew her chin-length brown hair out of her face with a frustrated huff. "What I could have *really used* was to have a grandfather in my life. I doubt there are any pleasant surprises in that will, Mr. Everett. And in all honesty, I'm starting not to care."

She seemed so weary and bitter, Gabe found himself amazed Darcy had gotten her here at all. "What if it's enough money to get you well settled with the girls?"

"Who says I'm not well settled in Tennessee? I have a job, Mr. Everett. I have clients and decorating jobs waiting on my return. We have a house in Dickson. It may not seem like much to a big rancher like you, but it's the place the girls have known all their lives. I can't imagine needing whatever is in that will."

He noticed she had not mentioned friends or family. And she'd said *house* not *home*. Avery Culpepper might not have much, but she surely had her pride. "Please stay," he said as congenially as he knew how. "I know it's asking a lot, but lots of boys' welfare depends on us meeting the requirements of your grandfather's will. And you're one of those requirements, even though I know that doesn't sit well with you."

"You're right. It doesn't."

"Haven's full of good people. Kind folks I know would help with the girls while you're here and all." He was desperate for any argument that would convince the woman not to head back to Tennessee.

Exhaustion pulled at her pretty features. His mother had worn herself thin trying to raise him all on her own, and there had been only *one* of him. Almost every memory he held of his mother contained the same bone-tired countenance Avery Culpepper now wore. The pain that singed her brown eyes told him she was feeling alone, used and overwhelmed.

Could he really blame her for being ready to put the drama of Haven behind her? Her estranged grandfather, Cyrus Culpepper—who was evidently just as ornery on both sides of the grave—had ignored her all her life only to demand her appearance now. Half the town had been on a wild-goose chase to find her and bring her here. And to receive what? So far Cyrus had bequeathed her just a run-down cabin. True to Cyrus, he'd hinted that there might be more. Only how *much* more—and what—was anybody's guess until they opened a designated envelope at the seventieth anniversary celebration of the boys ranch a few weeks from now.

An unusable half an inheritance with a commanded appearance for a mystery other half—that was pure Cyrus. It was just like him to pull some ridiculous stunt as a final goodbye to the town that had put up with his bullheadedness all his life.

Gabe hated having to plead with this poor young woman. Was Cyrus fool enough to think an inheritance could make up for years of being ignored? At least Gabe had a mom—even if it was a tired one; Avery had been shuttled from foster home to foster home from what he'd heard.

No, Avery had dozens of reasons not to go along with that old curmudgeon's ridiculous set of final demands. Only Gabe didn't have the luxury of her refusal.

The eyes of the ranch's residents—problem kids through little fault of their own, just like he'd been—seemed to stare down the back of his neck as if the boys stood behind him. *Tomorrow is March 1.* The clock was ticking on the March 20th deadline for the anniversary celebration. *Keep her here. Do whatever it takes.* Grinding his teeth, angry that a coot like Culpepper could still stir up such trouble from the grave, Gabe tried again. "Please say you'll stay. Just until we get this all straightened out. We'll all pitch in to make it as easy on you as possible." He hated that it sounded like he was begging. He hated even more that he *was* begging.

"I don't know." She didn't look at all convinced. She was barely paying him any attention with the wiggly girls skipping all around the porch as they played some noisy singsong of a game. Mercy, but there was a good reason he'd never married or started a family. Gabe's fingers twitched as if he could reach out and grab Cyrus's spindly neck and shake the endless meanness from the man. "Honestly," she continued as she grabbed Debbie just before the girls started skipping in circles around each other. "I just can't see how…"

The porch door swung open and a very irritated Roz Sackett emerged holding a frilly doll. *Oh, no.* Roz owned the boardinghouse, and her doll collection was her pride and joy. Everyone in town knew it. Everyone also knew Roz was not a woman known for grace or patience. One look at the colored smears on the doll's china face told Gabe that Roz had reached the end of her already-short fuse.

"Miss Avery," the innkeeper began in a clipped

tone, "I've told you more than once to keep those girls away from my collection."

At the sight of what was evidently her handiwork, Dinah left her skipping to head over toward the delicate doll. "She's pretty. Can I hold her?" Gabe grabbed the girl before she could reach her target. Nobody dared mess with Roz's precious doll collection—but Debbie and Dinah didn't know that.

Debbie, not to be bested by her sister, squealed, "Me first!" and darted around the table, rocking it and sending more markers rolling out over the porch floor.

Roz cried out in alarm, holding the doll above her head as if the thing was in mortal danger. While still holding Dinah by one elbow, Gabe managed to wedge a leg in front of Debbie. He'd hoped to simply impede her progress, but ended up tripping her instead, which sent her to the porch floor in tears. Naturally, Dinah began to cry, as well.

"I'm so sorry, Mrs. Sackett," Avery called over the increasing wails as she ducked around Gabe to reach Dinah and pick up Debbie. "It won't happen again."

"Oh, yes, it will," countered Roz as she continued to hold up the doll, out of little hands' reach. "Bless your heart, child, I know you've got your hands full, but this simply won't work. They're too rambunctious." Given everything that had just happened, Gabe found himself surprised Roz hadn't called the girls flat-out wild. "I'm at my wit's end!" the innkeeper declared, throwing up her free hand.

She wasn't wrong. The girls *were* wild. That wasn't necessarily Avery's fault. From what Gabe knew about four-year-olds—which was next to nothing since the youngest guests of the boys ranch were in first grade—preschoolers didn't come any other way but rambunctious.

Avery's eyes went narrow with hurt. "Well, I suppose we'll just have to head back to Dickson."

Gabe threw Roz a look he hoped said "we can't let her leave." The Blue Bonnet Inn—the only other place in Haven to stay—was full up and, as fancy as it was, would be no place for these youngsters.

Roz threw back an exasperated glare. "Well, I'm sorry to say it, but you can't stay here." She didn't look one bit sorry to have said it. Avery Culpepper didn't need anyone handing her reasons to leave. Didn't Roz realize half the town had been working toward meeting Culpepper's absurd ultimatums—which meant finding Avery and keeping her here—since October?

Do something. Anything. It jumped out of his mouth before he had even a moment to think better of it, the foolish notion of a desperate man. "You don't need to head back. You can come stay at Five Rocks."

Roz Sackett's eyebrows nearly popped through her hairline at the offer. If a face could shout impropriety for no good reason, it was hers.

"With me *and Jethro and Marlene,*" he clarified immediately, adjusting his hat, which had gone askew in the mayhem. "My housekeeper and her husband live on my ranch with me, remember?"

"Stay with you?" Avery looked shocked. She ought to. He was still shocked he'd made the offer at all.

"No," Gabe clarified a second time, "with me, my housekeeper and her husband." When both Avery and Mrs. Sackett still stared at him, he reached down and began gathering the markers off the floor. "If nothing else, four adults might give you a fighting chance against these two."

Debbie reached over and began picking up markers herself, but ended up knocking Gabe's hat off his head.

They all fell into stunned silence. No one, especially not a preschooler, knocked a cowboy's hat off his head. Gabe felt his face tighten into a frustrated scowl before he could stop it. Debbie, cued by his frown, caught on to the grievous nature of what she'd just done. Her bitty blue eyes went wide, the tiny pink lip below them jutted and quivered, and she dissolved once again into tears.

Gabriel Everett now added host to his list of demanding jobs—and it was the one that just might be the death of him.

Avery was sure she looked exasperated. Mostly because she was. Some days it felt like she hadn't known a moment's peace since Danny left.

No one should have to raise two precious little girls on her own. Debbie and Dinah should know their father, should see every day how much daddies loved mommies. How could any man she had been so sure she loved be capable of what Danny had done? Just up and decide that two children at once were too much? Had all his "faith" been false? He'd never been overly free with affection, but lately she wondered if he'd ever really loved her at all. Did the man ever give a thought to his dear daughters and how they fared?

Only her pride made her go on about *needing* to get back to Tennessee. Dickson was where she lived, where she was trying to make a life without Danny, but the truth was, precious little was back there. A house, a smattering of clients, some acquaintances, but no true friends.

Not that she'd admit any of that to anyone here. Successful businesswomen didn't up and leave their enterprises for weeks at a time to help with some charity case. She'd end up a charity case herself if she kept that up. Every eye in Haven seemed to stare at her in either expectation or suspicion. And as for the whole town being ready to help, she didn't much believe that. Not after Mrs. Sackett's persnickety scrutiny.

"Avery?" Gabe was clearly expecting an answer to his startlingly generous offer. It was clear he would do anything to get her to stay, and the pressure of that choked any reply.

Life had dropped too many emotional bombs since her arrival here to let her think clearly. Coming to Haven had felt like stepping into a crammed-full kind of chaos. Really, who ever discovers they've been impersonated? Some gold-digging woman had actually come here earlier claiming to be her. Clearly, she was supposed to be someone important. The whole town was in an uproar over the fate of her grandfather Cyrus's estate. It had been set—along with a mountain of stipulations, one of which included her presence—to become the new home of a ranch for troubled boys. The huge house went to a worthy cause, while she, evidently his only surviving relative, got a run-down cabin. Everyone wanted something from her despite the fact that she was just trying to hold her life together. Someone important? Ha! The number of nights she fell into bed exhausted and near tears ought to be illegal.

Should she stay? *Could* she stay?

"You're serious?" she finally asked Gabe as she tried unsuccessfully to fetch the poor man's toppled hat. "I mean…look at them." She loved Dinah and Debbie to pieces, but even she knew they could be a handful. Gabriel Everett did not seem at all like the kind of man who would suffer any children—much less four-year-olds—with any grace.

Time came to a prickly halt while the man bent over, grasped his hat and settled it back on his head. He seemed as shocked at the proposition he'd just made as she was.

"Marlene will love them," he said almost begrudgingly. "She and Jethro have their grandkids in college now, and Marlene needs someone to coddle. I caught her staring at an ad for puppies the other day." Avery got the distinct impression he was trying to convince himself as much as her.

"No, I'd expect it would be best if we just went back."

"You can't." He wiped his hands down his face. "I mean, the whole town would be obliged if you'd stay. I've got the space, and things aren't so—" he gestured around the boardinghouse "—fussy out there. Not much they could break or stain."

Dinah and Debbie had indeed excelled at breaking and staining recently. Mrs. Sackett hadn't asked her to pay for or replace anything the girls had damaged, but she could tell the woman was getting close to drawing up a bill. The dolls—which they had been warned about several times—were clearly the last straw.

Would it be so awful to stay a bit longer? At a place with extra helping hands? Experienced grandparent hands? "Well," Avery said, pulling in a deep breath, "I suppose we could give it a try."

Avery's eye caught Mrs. Sackett's hard stare, one that practically shouted "you sure as shooting better give it a try."

Stay with Gabriel Everett?

Help with the girls was a hard prospect to refuse right about now, even though Haven wasn't turning out anything like she'd hoped.

"How soon can you take them, Gabe?" Mrs. Sackett asked with a hurtful sense of urgency. Clearly, she meant every word of her threat to toss them out.

"Well, it's Monday. I think I can have them off your hands by tomorrow noon, Roz. Just a matter of a phone call and a bit of rearranging." He turned to look at Avery. "If that's agreeable to you."

"Well, then, I guess I should thank you kindly for the hospitality," she said, handing markers to Dinah to put back in the box. Just like that, the girls went back to their coloring. Her sweet little girls had returned— at least until the next calamity.

But something needed to be said. "Just for a week or so. Maybe less. I haven't made up my mind about anything after that." She'd gotten the distinct impression that being a Culpepper wasn't a positive in this town—nothing she wanted a big dose of, for her or the girls.

"Let's tackle that subject in a day or two." Gabriel turned his gaze to the innkeeper again. "After all, we can't have you run out of town now, can we?"

Mrs. Sackett just huffed, held the doll close to her

chest as if the thing was alive and turned back toward the door.

"I don't know." Resentment at Cyrus for putting her in this position boiled in her blood—right now she could barely bring herself to care about whatever else the old man was leaving her, if anything.

Avery reached down to touch Dinah's soft brown curls. "They're not difficult all the time, you know. They really can be sweet as pie some days."

Gabe returned an orange marker to the table. "I'm sure that's true." He didn't look like he meant it.

"I'm sure the boys ranch is a fine cause, but I need to think about what's best for the girls, and for me." Avery hated how tight and forced her voice sounded.

"No one can fault you for that. Just take some time before you decide." He stuffed his hands in his pockets, looking down at the little girls with a mixture of bafflement and irritation. "Give us a chance to work all this out."

She didn't have it in her to fight. At least not today. "We'll see."

It wasn't a yes, but he looked relieved anyway. "I'll come by tomorrow around eleven and we can load my truck with whatever doesn't fit in your car. I'll call Marlene right now. I'm sure it'll set her into a storm of happy preparations. Is it okay if I give her your phone number if she has any questions?"

"Sure." The prospect of getting out of the boardinghouse lifted a weight off Avery's shoulders she hadn't even realized was pressing down so hard. "Thank you," she said, fighting the awkward and indebted feeling that settled cold and hard against her rigid spine. "Really. It's a very kind offer."

Gabriel shrugged. "I've got the space, and nothing gets solved if you leave. It works for everybody." He seemed more at peace with the idea than he had been even two minutes ago.

That peace wasn't likely to last. "We'll see if you say that after twenty-four hours of these two, cowboy," Avery teased. He couldn't really know what he was getting himself into, could he?

"I've handled far rougher bulls at the ranch. How hard can a pair of little girls be?"

Bless his heart, Avery thought, *he's about to find out.*

Chapter Two

Following a mountain of exasperating Lone Star Cowboy League business, Gabe came home that Monday afternoon to find Marlene and Jethro Frank cleaning a batch of old toys. Even the squeal of joy Marlene had given over the phone hadn't prepared him for just how much the older couple was going to enjoy this spontaneous setup. As he cut the ignition on his truck, Gabe couldn't help but wonder if he was looking at his last quiet evening on the ranch for a while.

"Evening, Gabriel," Jethro called from over a bucket of sudsy water. "Just getting things ready."

Gabe looked to his left to see child-sized pastel sheets hanging on the line. "You had all this?"

"A few calls around church was all it took," Marlene said with a smile. She chuckled as she handed a bright green doll carriage to Jethro. "Little girls! And twins at that!"

Jethro shot Gabe just a hint of a "you sure you know what you're doing?" glance, one gray eyebrow raised as he plunged a sponge into the soapy water.

Gabe had no idea what he was doing. He'd been asking himself all afternoon what on earth had made him offer to house Avery and the twins. He didn't especially like children—but he liked failing a whole town even less.

It wasn't as if life hadn't complicated itself tenfold in the past few months. Cyrus's will was forcing him to hunt down Theodore Linley, his maternal grandfather—someone Gabe never wanted to see again. Worse yet, Linley clearly didn't want to be found. No one else in Haven had been able to locate him, and even the private investigators hired to find the man had failed.

Cyrus Culpepper's set of demands was beginning to look more impossible with each passing day.

Desperation, he decided. That's what made him do it. The desperation he felt to save the boys ranch from losing the larger facilities it so dearly needed.

If necessity was the mother of invention, it seemed desperation was the father of foolishness.

"Supper's in the slow cooker," Marlene called as Gabe pulled his briefcase from the truck. His stomach growled at the mention of supper—Gabe hadn't had time to eat lunch today. He'd spent the time after seeing Avery in an endless stream of appointments for his role as president of the Lone Star Cowboy League's Waco chapter. The civic organization did important work supporting area ranchers, but lately it seemed the league devoured all his time. Gabe was a highly organized and precise man, and the length of his list of undone tasks was making him nuts. "We'll eat in thirty minutes," Marlene advised. "We've got enough for Harley, if you want to fetch him over."

Harley Jones was an old ranch hand who had been

here since Gabe's stepfather owned the ranch. Gabe could never bear to put him off the property, even though the man had long outlived his usefulness.

Much as he liked Harley, Gabe was too tired and hungry for extra faces around the table tonight. In fact, if he thought Marlene would let him get away with it, he'd prefer to spend the evening eating at his desk, working through the pile of emails and other documents that still needed tending today. "Put some in the freezer and I'll drop a pot of leftovers over on Friday." Gabe grinned at his cleverness—it might serve him good to pile up a bunch of reasons to visit Harley and escape the house once those girls descended.

Marlene cooed at a doll she had plucked from a box. "Your mail's on your desk."

"Thanks. Did you manage to make it out for extra groceries?" he asked as he walked up his ranch house's wide front porch. The house was expansive—"too large for one man alone" Marlene never stopped saying. He would always point out that he wasn't alone— he had her and Jethro—but she would just scowl and give him a "you know what I mean" motherly glare.

On his worse days, Gabe called her Meddling Marlene. On his better days, he tolerated her attempts to fix up his life as well as his house with a begrudging affection. Much as he preferred solitude, the Franks were good company. Big-hearted people, faithful, loyal and kind. What would the state of that beloved solitude be after the three weeks he needed Avery to stay? Shredded, no doubt, but the boys ranch was worth the price.

"We stocked up at the store," Jethro informed him. "Marlene's baked cookies already."

Gabe's stomach paid attention to those words. "Cookies?"

"Gingerbread," Marlene said. "You don't want something too sugary with little ones in the house."

Marlene had better be more worried about her cookie jar being raided by the *big* guy in the house. "Better hide those cookies," Gabe teased as he pulled open the door. "I've always liked gingerbread."

"I knew that," Marlene declared. "Why do you think I made a double batch? No sneaking till after supper, Gabriel."

Gabe laughed, but detoured through the kitchen to what he knew to be Marlene's hiding spot. He grabbed half a dozen of the delicious-smelling goodies before dragging himself to his desk. Only a fool would attack the mail on an empty stomach, he justified.

On top of his far-too-tall stack of mail was a hand-addressed envelope from Mike Tower. Gabe smiled as he broke the seal to open an invitation to Mike's thirty-fifth birthday party in Houston.

That's why I'm doing this. Mike had been a best friend during Gabe's years at the boys ranch. They'd both had tough starts in life, but turned out fine. Gabe ran a prosperous ranch and was president of the Lone Star Cowboy League. Mike ran one of Houston's top law firms. The boys ranch turned lives around and deserved to expand. If he had to suffer a pair of little girls for three weeks—*three weeks*! He surely hadn't thought this through carefully—to ensure that the ranch could continue its good work, he could ride it out.

He started to fill out the reply card, then changed his mind and picked up the phone. The mountain of mail could wait another five minutes.

"Howdy there, Gabe!" The sound of a squalling baby filled the air behind Mike's distinctive drawl.

"Caught you at a bad time, did I?"

"It's Terri's night out with the girls. Me and Mikey are just a couple of happy bachelors tonight."

Gabe winced at the weariness that tugged at the corners of Mike's joke. "One of you fellas doesn't sound too happy."

"Teething," moaned the new father. "I'll never take a set of pearly whites for granted ever again. My little buckaroo's been miserable for days, and he's taken Terri right down with him. She needed to get out of Dodge tonight, that's for sure, and I'm coming to realize why." As if to underscore Mike's point, Mikey let out an enthusiastic howl.

Gabe tried to imagine the halls of Five Rocks Ranch reverberating with a pair of such howls. Just the five minutes of crying on Roz's porch had set his nerves on edge. Four-year-olds didn't cry as much as babies, did they? "I guess I should let you go, then."

"No, please," Mike begged above the wailing, "I need the human contact."

"Aren't lawyers humans?" Gabe replied with a laugh.

"Only barely. One of my cases has the staff in fits, so work isn't as much fun as usual. Speaking of fun, how are those investigators working out? My or Phillips's guys turned up anything on your grandfather yet?" Mike had added the best private investigators he knew to a set hired by local attorney Fletcher

Snowden Phillips. All in an effort to find Theodore. All without success. After today's complication, Gabe had a few choice words for the late Cyrus and his preposterous demands.

Gabe tossed his hat onto the bentwood coatrack that stood in the corner of his office. "Nothing past the jail term we knew about before. Honestly, Mike, it's like the guy disappeared into thin air. I hate having to hunt him down. The only good side to finding him is that I can finally give him a piece of my mind. What man gives his daughter the slip like that? Leaving Mom and me to scrape by in the world?"

Gabe tamped down the burn of resentment that rose too easily these days and eased himself into the big leather chair behind his desk. Right now he could see exactly why Avery might want to put Cyrus and all of Haven behind her. Not much in life stung worse than being abandoned by the family that was supposed to love and care for you.

He heard Mike's sigh above the baby's noisy cries. "Think of it this way. That's what makes the boys ranch so important. A boy can go so wrong so fast when he's ignored or abandoned."

"True, counselor." Gabe pinched the bridge of his nose and reached for a cookie.

"And that's why you've got to find him," Mike said. "It's up to you to ensure the boys ranch won't lose the chance to expand. That place can't be sold to a strip mall and half those kids sent elsewhere. You and I both know that."

"I know, I know. And I've gone to extremes, Mike, believe me."

"How so?"

"I invited the real Avery and her girls to stay here since Roz Sackett was fixing to kick them out of the boardinghouse on account of their 'rambunctiousness.'"

"You what?" Mike was understandably shocked at a move so far out of character for Gabe.

"You remember Roz Sackett."

"I remember she can be mean."

"Mean enough to hand Avery a reason to head back to Tennessee and keep us from our goal. Who boots out a single mom with a pair of four-year-olds?"

"Wait a minute," Mike said, nearly laughing. "You mean to tell me you invited *children* to stay at *your* house? Just how pretty is this single mama?"

Avery Culpepper was pretty, but that didn't have anything to do with it. Even the prettiest mom, if she came with kids in tow, wasn't for him. Gabe was many things, but a family man hadn't ever been one of them. He'd stayed a bachelor all his years by choice, thank you. "I had to keep her from heading out of town, Mike. She's got to stay for the seventieth anniversary party—you know it's one of Cyrus's cockamamy demands. I was fresh out of options."

"I'll say. Boy howdy, I'd like to see you with a pair of little girls pulling on your pant legs. Sounds entertaining."

"About as entertaining as that opera singer you got there," Gabe joked back. Every minute Mikey kept up the crying dug a deeper hole of doubt regarding what he'd just done in offering his own home. Little girls. What had come over him?

"You coming to my party?" Mike asked. "I mean, if you live that long?"

"Wouldn't miss it for the world," Gabe growled, thinking it would have been far smarter to just fill out the reply card.

"Good," Mike replied. "Say, when do the kiddos move in?"

"Tomorrow afternoon."

Mike laughed. "I'll call you Thursday and see if you're still standing. Let me know if my guys find your grandpappy. Sure would be nice if this whole circus actually worked out, but then again, this is Cyrus we're talking about. Anything could happen."

"Don't I know it. Cowboy up and get through the night watch, okay? I'm worried about you."

"Don't you worry about me," Mike responded with a weary laugh. "I'm not the one about to be surrounded by females."

Gabe ended the call with the sinking feeling that Mike was all too right.

"This place is huge." Avery stared down the long hallway that led to the pair of rooms she and the girls would occupy. They had their own wing, which was practically the size of their house in Tennessee. Back at the boardinghouse, they'd been all stuffed into one room with a bathroom down the hall. Avery felt like she hadn't had the space to take a deep breath since she came to town.

Marlene, Gabe's wonderfully friendly housekeeper, put an encouraging hand on Avery's shoulder. "We've definitely got room to spare, honey. I'm so glad you took Gabriel up on his offer." The woman was a natural-born grandmother if ever there was one. The girls had taken to her and her husband, Jethro, instantly. Of course, the freshly baked gingerbread cookies may have had a great deal to do with that, but right now she didn't care. This place felt miles better than where they had been, and Marlene felt like desperately needed support.

Debbie raced past them, nearly knocking the housekeeper over as she catapulted into the room and flung herself onto one of the two small beds. In seconds Dinah was right behind her, flopping with a squeal onto the bright pink gingham sheets that topped each bed.

"Everything's so pink, Mama!" Dinah called, arms and legs flailing in little girl delight.

Marlene chuckled. "What little girl doesn't love pink?" She gave Avery a knowing look. "You've got your hands full, bless your heart."

If I had a dime for every time I heard that, Avery thought. She did hear it all the time. Everyone always said it back in Tennessee, but folks rarely lent a hand to help with the twins. Avery sighed. "I do indeed. I'm sorry for the racket."

"Don't you be one bit sorry. Five Rocks is a big and beautiful place, but I've always found it far too quiet. Oh, I know Gabriel says he likes his peace and order, but I think it'll be nice to have some happy noise around for a change," Marlene said as she walked into the room. "Now," she said, pointing to one girl, "are you Dinah or are you Debbie? I'm gonna have trouble keeping you two straight."

Any version of the "who's who?" game sent Debbie into peals of laughter. "I'm Debbie," she said, rolling over to grin at Marlene and point at her dark hair.

"Well, I'm glad for that hair," Marlene said as she

eased herself onto Debbie's bed. "I need all the hints I can get. Tell me, Debbie, are you ready for lunch? I have bologna sandwiches cut out into heart shapes with carrots and sweet, juicy peaches."

"Dinah's a notoriously picky eater," Avery offered from the doorway, hoping to spare dear Mrs. Frank one of Dinah's all-too-frequent mealtime tantrums.

"Oh, that don't scare me none. I raised three sons and five grandchildren. I've seen it all." She winked at Avery. "This grandma's got a few tricks up her sleeve."

Avery couldn't help herself. "Use any on Gabe?"

Marlene gave a hearty laugh. "Don't tell. It works best if we let him think he's in charge."

"That's because I am." Gabe's voice came from the hallway behind Avery. His dark eyebrows furrowed down over the man's astonishingly blue eyes as he peered into the room. "Where'd all this come from?"

"Rhetta's twins outgrew their beds last year. Jethro went over and borrowed them early this morning."

"It's a whole lot of princess pink!" Dinah called with glee.

"I'll say," Gabe said, wincing. "My teeth hurt just looking at it."

"Girls, you should say thank you to…" Avery stopped, realizing she wasn't quite sure how to finish that sentence. "What do you want them to call you?"

It seemed like a land mine of a question. Gabriel Everett was an imposing figure of a man. Tall and dark-haired with strong, solid features, he certainly wasn't the "Uncle Gabe" type. Not even "Mr. Gabe." Still, Mr. Everett sounded like a mouthful for a four-year-old.

"Do they have to call me anything?" Gabe seemed to find the question just as daunting.

"Well, of course they do," Marlene said.

Gabe gave a bit of a twitch, as if he'd just realized housing the girls was going to mean he'd have to *actually talk* to them on occasion. Avery would have classified his behavior yesterday as an awkward tolerance—or perhaps it was more of a cornered surrender, now that she thought about it. The discomfort seemed to grow larger as Gabe scratched his chin and considered how the girls should address him. "Mr. Everett?" he offered halfheartedly, as if he couldn't come up with anything better.

Avery was afraid he'd say that. She really didn't think she could refuse, so she was especially glad when Marlene countered, "Don't you think that's a bit formal for someone their age?" The housekeeper shot a disapproving look Gabe's way.

Avery was wracking her brains for a suitable moniker when Debbie bounced off the bed and walked right up to Gabe with the air of a woman in possession of the solution. "Boots," she declared, pointing to Gabe's large brown cowboy boots.

Gabe looked around, waiting for someone to pronounce what a bad idea that was.

"You can be Mr. Boots!" Debbie said again, this time squatting down to pat her hand up against the dusty leather.

Dinah, not to be outdone, slid off her bed and began to chant "Mr. Boots" while pointing at Gabe's other leg. Poor Gabe, he'd been christened against his will now; once the girls latched on to something like this, they rarely let go.

"Could have been worse," Marlene offered with a grin that broadcast just how much she was enjoying this. "They might have picked 'Mr. Scowl.'"

Avery felt like she had to at least try. "Don't you think you girls could learn to say 'Mr. Everett'?"

In reply, the girls only chanted "Mr. Boots!" louder.

"Um, I'll try to keep that down to a minimum," she said above the noise as the girls began to circle around Gabe's legs like little pink cats, patting Gabe's boots while he stood there in mild shock and not-so-mild annoyance.

Avery was composing a suitable apology when Gabe just seemed to shrug and resign himself to the new nickname. "I've been called worse."

The man was huge and intimidating—she didn't doubt he'd been called a great deal of things. Only right now, she called him her host, and that deserved whatever kindness she could provide. "If it helps, I promise *I'll* never use it." It seemed slim consolation to a man whose spare bedroom had just been transformed into a tidal wave of pink gingham.

Gabe stuffed his hands in his pockets. "Well, I'd be much obliged for that."

"Well, *I'm* making no such promises," Marlene offered with a wink and a grin. "I rather like 'Mr. Boots.'"

Gabe gave her a dark look and carefully extracted his long legs from the girls' endless circles. "I've got to return a couple of calls, ladies. Marlene, how long before lunch?"

"We were just discussing lunch now. It'll be ready in twenty minutes. So no cookies." Marlene slanted a sideways glance at Avery. "That man always sneaks food into his office."

"Too late!" Gabe called, and Avery caught sight of the man producing a stack of cookies from his shirt pocket and waving them in the air like a schoolboy who'd just gotten away with a prank. Clearly, Marlene and Gabe one-upped each other on a continual basis.

Such behavior didn't fit the domineering, driven Gabriel Everett she'd met on her first day in Haven. That man was bent on getting what he needed, pressing for her compliance, pushing hard for whatever it took to secure the boys ranch. His own ranch was huge and clearly prosperous—those sorts of businessmen didn't sneak cookies or open their homes to little girls.

Of course, Gabe Everett had opened his home because he needed something from her—she knew that. He hosted to keep her from leaving because he needed her here for the celebration. Cyrus's will stipulated that she, as well as the three other original residents of the Lone Star Cowboy League Boys Ranch, had to be present on March 20. If not, the property left to the ranch would be sold to a strip mall, which would send half the ranch's current residents elsewhere. *Well*, she told herself as she led Dinah and Debbie to the bathroom to wash up for lunch, *if I'm going to be stuck between a rock and a hard place, at least the hard place is looking nicer every minute.*

Chapter Three

"I hate him, you know."

Gabe looked at Avery later that evening as she stood on the porch watching the stars come out. Jethro had taken the girls inside to read them one of his cowboy stories—Jethro had written down stories for as long as Gabe could remember, and was taking full advantage of his tiny new audience. The quiet of the falling dusk was as thick as a blanket after the commotion of moving-in day. Gabe felt like he could exhale for the first time since that wild meeting on Roz's porch.

"Who?" Gabe replied. He had a notion who she meant, since she'd just refused a tour of the ranch— her grandfather's home—but felt he ought to ask anyway.

"Grandpa Cyrus. Well, Cyrus Culpepper to all of you. Even before I knew who he was, I hated him."

Between the imposter Avery and the real Avery, Gabe was having trouble keeping his Cyrus stories straight. "I thought you never knew Cyrus." Of course, Gabe knew *knowing* didn't really come into a situation like this—he, of all people, knew how easy it was to hate someone you'd barely known. In fact, it was almost easier to hate the *idea* of someone than to hate an actual person. He resented his own grandfather deeply for abandoning him at a young age; it wasn't hard to believe Avery felt the same.

"Daddy would always say that if things went bad, Grandpa would come and save us. 'Grandpa will do this' and 'Grandpa will do that.'" She turned to look at Gabe, pain filling her eyes. "I know I was only six, but I remember the promises. And I waited. After Daddy died, I waited in one foster home after another. Only Grandpa never came. Never. That man never did a single thing to help me." Her words were sharp and bitter.

"You're sure? I mean, he could have been trying." Gabe remembered harboring the silly hope that somehow his own grandfather had tried valiantly to get in touch with Mom. He made up all kinds of reasons how their many moves had stumped Grandpa Theo's efforts. After a while, the hard truth of his abandonment won out over the optimism of such stories. Gabe knew what a hollow space that left.

Avery turned to look at him. "That'd make a nice story, wouldn't it? Only no. The foster service tried multiple times to find him and reach him. They had contact information for him. No one ever answered." She hugged herself, shoulders bunching up. A sore point to be sure, and who could blame her?

"That must have been hard," Gabe offered.

She didn't answer, simply nodded.

"I'm sorry," he tried again, even though it felt intrusive and inadequate. Gabe was all too familiar with how rejection brewed a slow, sour kind of pain,

one that was deep and hard to shake. "I think maybe
Cyrus regretted it in the end, if that helps."

She gave a lifeless laugh. "It doesn't."

Gabe walked over beside her, putting one boot
up on the lower rung of the porch rail. It made him
think of the chorus of "Mr. Boots!" he'd heard all
afternoon, and he felt the surprise of a smile curl up
the corners of his mouth. "It's why the boys ranch is
so important, you know."

"The bumper crop of lousy parents in the world?"

It was becoming clear that Avery Culpepper rarely
minced words. In that way, she was a lot like her
grandfather—not that he'd be foolish enough to point
that out at the moment. "Sure, some parents are lousy,"
Gabe replied. "Some are just gone. And some just
plain don't have it in them. More helpless than mean."

"No one has the right to abandon a child. I'd bleed
to the last drop before I'd walk away from my girls."
She didn't say "like their father did," but Gabe felt it
hang in the air just the same.

"That's the way it should be. Only it doesn't always
happen that way, does it? The kids at the ranch did
nothing wrong—well, some of them have acted out
in bad ways, but you know what I mean. They didn't
set their lives up badly, but things haven't worked out
for them just the same. And that's not fair."

"I suppose not. I never felt much of life was fair,
to tell you the truth."

"It isn't. That's what keeps me working for the boys
ranch. Every boy we house and counsel is one less
man who grows up hauling a ball of hate around."
Even as he spoke the words, Gabe wondered if he really believed them. After all, he'd been a resident at

the ranch some twenty-odd years ago, and the ball of hate was still following him around like a lead shadow.

Avery leaned up against the thick porch column, her arms still wrapped around her chest. "I didn't ask to be the only thing saving the Culpepper land from becoming a strip mall. I can't say for certain that I can stay all the way until the twentieth."

"I understand you need to do what's best for you and your girls. But that doesn't change how much we need your cooperation. Think about it this way—if you'd had a girls ranch to go to instead of that long string of foster homes, would things have turned out differently for you?"

She didn't reply, which told Gabe he'd perhaps made his point, so he went on. "The boys ranch is a good thing. It's worth expanding." Gabe planted his hands on top of the porch rail and looked out in the direction where the ranch lay beyond a line of trees. If he could just get her there, even once, it would help to convince her.

"And while I wish old Cyrus would have been nice enough to help that without all these hijinks, I've got to take his help the way it came."

Avery's dark laugh returned. "'Hijinks.' That's one way to put it." She ran one hand through the neat fringe of brown hair that framed her round face. "You know, those messages and emails from Darcy Hill just about knocked me over. I didn't know what to think. It's a crazy scheme, even you have to admit that. I only decided to come on the hopes I'd get some answers. Or maybe I came half out of curiosity. Or amusement." She paused for a long moment, then added, "I didn't count on it hurting so much, you know?"

Gabe shifted his gaze to her, startled by the admission. "How so?"

"To walk around here and see this picture postcard of a little town. To know I could have been here rather than those dumps of foster homes if only he'd…" Her words fell off and she turned away. "Like I said, I know it's not very Christian of me, but I hate him."

Up until this moment, Gabe hadn't been able to fathom what would allow Avery to walk away from a possible inheritance. Here he'd thought it was just the frustration of living under Roz Sackett's glare, that getting her here would solve everything and be worth the chaos he'd just launched upon his household.

That wasn't the half of it. What was eating Avery Culpepper was so much more than just squirrelly twins. Cyrus Culpepper cast a long, cold shadow here in Haven, and he couldn't blame her for not wanting to spend any time in it. Neither her nor her girls. It was, as Pastor Walsh would put it, "a God-sized problem" of history and pain.

History and pain. The world was flooded with it. He'd lived it, she'd lived it. The boys ranch fought against it, one young life at a time. *How do I solve this, Lord? How can I override twenty years of a dead man's neglect? I've got to find a way.* Gabe pleaded to the heaven he'd once imagined hid behind the veil of stars. Somehow he'd have to convince this woman to set aside the mountain of pride and pain she clearly carried while trying to make his own grandfather appear out of thin air.

A God-sized problem indeed.

* * *

Avery groped her way toward the kitchen coffee-maker Wednesday morning, every bone aching from lack of sleep. How had the girls managed to be so sleepless and fidgety well into the wee hours after such an eventful day?

"Oh, dear," said Marlene as she stood slicing bread at the counter. "You don't look like you've slept a wink."

"I think it was three…four, maybe, by the time the both of them finally nodded off for good." Avery didn't even have the energy to stifle her yawn. "I thought they'd be exhausted. I sure am."

Marlene looked crestfallen. "They didn't like their beds?"

"Oh, they love them. I think the changes of location keep knocking them for a bit of a loop. By one a.m. I had both of them crawling in bed with me, all kicking and sprawling and fidgety." She spooned sugar into the strong-smelling brew. "It was like sleeping with a pair of mules on espresso."

That made Marlene laugh. "I was sure Jethro and I had worn them out. We tried."

The older couple really had gone out of their way to play with Dinah and Debbie, especially after supper, when Avery felt drained from the stresses of the day. "At least they're still out cold, the little darlings. My bed is up against the wall, so when I smelled coffee, I propped up a few pillows on the open edge and slipped out. I'm hoping that will buy me at least five minutes to grab a cup."

"Oh, honey, the way you look I ought to send you

out to the porch swing with a thermos and a blanket. Young ones take so much out of you, don't they?"

Avery sipped the coffee, letting the bracing hot brew pull her toward clarity. The coffee at the boardinghouse was passable, but this coffee was marvelous. And not all the way down a flight of stairs, where she didn't feel right leaving the girls. She wrapped her hands around the stoneware mug and breathed a sigh of gratitude. A cup of morning coffee in quiet felt like the grandest of luxuries. "I wouldn't trade them for the world," Avery answered the housekeeper, "even when they stomp on my last nerve."

"And we all know little ones can surely do that." Marlene put a compassionate hand on Avery's shoulder. "I'm glad you're here. Truly."

"I hope Gabe can say the same." Avery ran her hands through what must be a bird's nest of bed hair. "Where is he?"

"Off into Waco on business bright and early this morning. That man has risen before the sun every day I've known him. If you like the coffee, you can thank him—he makes it before the rest of us even open our eyes."

Her mind concocted a vision of Gabe vaulting into his truck and peeling down the gravel road, eager to escape the girlish invasion. It would have been smarter to refuse his offer. He must be regretting it after yesterday's chaos, but he'd been a gentleman and hidden any sign of it. Either that or the boys ranch must be truly desperate to win her compliance.

The discomfort must have shown on her face, for Marlene squeezed her shoulder. "Oh, I know Gabriel can look like a stiff old bull sometimes, but he's got a heart of gold down under it all. It'll work out just fine, I promise you. Just takes a little adjusting."

Avery leaned up against the counter. "What I don't get is, why did he make the offer in the first place?"

"Well, you know the obvious reason."

Avery put her hand to her forehead. "My grandfather and his kooky demands."

Marlene sighed. "That old coot was a puzzle if ever there was one. Kept to himself mostly, and grumbled when he did speak up. You could have knocked me over with a feather when Gabriel told me about his bequest." She straightened up suddenly. "Listen to me talking ill of the deceased. Forgive me."

Avery glanced up from her coffee. "That's just it, Marlene. He *wasn't* my grandfather. I mean he was, but I never really knew him. I was surprised when Darcy found me and sent those messages. I ignored them at first, thinking they were some kind of internet hoax. Then I got to thinking…" She let her words trail off. "I don't know what I got to thinking." Avery knew she was too tired to get into this now, but the words seemed to tumble out of her without permission.

Marlene's hand covered Avery's own. "This has to be hard, all the demands and the messy history. And that other Avery! You two are night and day—and I can't tell you how glad I am it's *you* who's the real granddaughter."

Avery had heard a few harrowing tales of the woman who preceded her into Haven claiming to be Cyrus Culpepper's flesh and blood. The kind folks called her things like "a piece of work" and "up to no good." Others had far harsher terms for the woman.

High heels, long nails, fancy cars? Avery thought she surely must look dumpy and unsuccessful when compared to that imposter! It just made everything in this crazy mess that much more complicated.

"I know Gabriel was downright relieved to know that other woman wasn't going to stay in Haven."

Avery didn't know how to answer. She wasn't going to stay in Haven, either.

Marlene clucked her tongue. "I wouldn't want that woman in this house, and Gabriel would have never made the offer, that's for sure."

Which brought the conversation around to Avery's original question. "Why did he offer to put us up? I don't get the sense he's fond of children."

Marlene let out a soft laugh. "Oh, he's not. Your girls stump him but good. Kind of entertaining, actually. His face when he saw those pink sheets? Priceless."

It would be amusing—if it wasn't so disconcerting—to see commanding Gabe Everett overrun by little people in pigtails. "All the more reason not to offer. I'm sure we could have found someplace else to go—if we chose to stay," Avery felt compelled to add. "Waited it out until there were rooms at the Blue Bonnet. Or convinced Mrs. Sackett to keep us on."

"If you couldn't contain the girls at the Haven Boardinghouse, they'd have been impossible at Carol's fancy Blue Bonnet place. And as for Roz Sackett? No one convinces that woman of anything but her own importance. Frankly, I'm amazed she put up with your sweet girls as long as she did." Marlene sipped her own coffee. "No, what got you here was Gabriel's determination to do whatever it took to save the boys ranch. Oh, I know he talks a good game, all serious and determined and the like, but if there's one thing that man can't resist, it's a good cause that needs saving."

Avery had no intention to be thought of as a cause that needed saving. She'd make it with the girls on her own without Danny. She'd head back to Tennessee when—or before—this was all over and give the girls a good life and fine futures.

"Comes from the way he was brought up, I expect," Marlene continued. "He and his mom went through some hard times. Makes him eager to give back now that he has so much." Marlene swung her hands around the large kitchen. "And so much space! This big old house practically echoes emptiness some nights. I'm glad for you and the girls. He will be, too, although don't hold your breath to hear him admit it. The girls will settle in, though, honey, you just watch. Why, in no time I expect—"

Her words were cut off by a loud crash, a tiny wail and the unmistakable sound of little feet running down the hallway floor. Avery practically tossed her coffee on the counter and ducked down the hallway to see Dinah tumbling at her with wide, frightened eyes. "Mama!"

"What's wrong, sweetheart?"

Dinah just buried her face in Avery's shoulder, clinging tight. "Mama. Mama. My pink's all gone. All the pink is gone."

It took a minute for Avery's undercaffeinated brain to process what Dinah was saying. "Your pink's not gone, sweetheart."

Dinah pulled away and rubbed her eyes while she looked at Avery. "I woke up and it was all gone." Her pout was as sweet as it was serious. Avery stood up, took Dinah's hand and began walking back toward their bedrooms. "It's still there. You and Debbie just crawled in bed with me last night. Look." She reached the girls' adjoining room and pushed the door open.

"My pink!" squealed Dinah, instantly joyful. She grabbed at the candy-colored sheets and turned to look at her mama. "I thought I dreamed it."

"Well, isn't she the sweetest thing ever," Marlene said from behind her. "Do you like cinnamon toast, Miss Dinah?"

"Cinnamon toast?" Dinah's eyes grew wide.

"I make the best cinnamon toast in the county. Want to try some for breakfast?"

Dinah nodded. "Ebbie, too?" When Dinah was sad or tired, she often dropped the *D* in her sister's name. Avery, who'd never had brothers or sisters, adored how her daughters always thought kindly of each other. Except when one had a toy the other one wanted, in which case kindness went out the window in a heartbeat.

Marlene smiled. "Why, of course Debbie gets some, too." She hunched down to Dinah's level. "Let's go roust her up, shall we?" She slanted her glance up toward Avery with a knowing grin. "That way your mama can have a long, hot shower while we eat our breakfast."

That, and the hot coffee, had Avery ready to nominate Marlene Frank for Woman of the Year. She'd have to find some friends like Marlene back in Tennessee. There had to be someone in Danny's hometown who didn't think she'd driven him off, who would believe that it was *he* who abandoned *them*.

The only home the girls had ever known was back there; she owed it to them to build her business up enough to make it work with Danny's alimony.

She was a fighter, always had been. Maybe she'd consider staying just long enough to see if Gabe was right and Cyrus really did leave her something worthwhile.

Chapter Four

Gabe knocked on the weather-beaten door of Harley Jones's small cottage on the west side of his ranch Friday morning. It was early, but Harley was an early riser like himself. The old man would be glad for the pot of hearty food, and Gabe liked to check in frequently on the widower's deteriorating health. "Harley?"

The sound of shuffling came from the other side of the door. "Hold your horses, I'm a'comin'."

The door creaked open, and Gabe made a mental note to bring oil on his next visit. Harley was trying to hold the place together on his own, but he needed help.

"Gabe." Harley pulled open the door, then hobbled on his cane back inside to the cabin's meager kitchen. "The league meeting's not today, is it?"

"Not today, Harley. I just thought you might help me finish off some of Marlene's good stew. She always makes enough to feed an army, and now with our—" Gabe groped for some way to describe Avery and her daughters' descent upon his quiet household "—houseguests, she's making even more."

He opened Harley's fridge, scanning the near-empty appliance as he settled the casserole dish Marlene had sent. Harley wasn't eating nearly as well as he should. Gabe made a note to visit again soon with some groceries. The pretense of escaping the noisy state of the ranch house would work well for everyone.

Not that he needed any incentive to visit Harley. Even as a young man on his stepfather's ranch—back when things were still tight, before Gabe stepped in as owner and made Five Rocks the prosperous ranch it was today—Gabe loved to spend time with Harley at this cabin. Leon, the last of Gabe's two stepfathers, had been a hard man who'd grown harder when Gabe's mother died.

Gabe warmed at the welcome sound of Harley putting on coffee—the old-fashioned way, in a blue enamel pot on a stove burner, never one of those "newfangled electric gizmos." Most of the happy memories Gabe had of his time on this ranch were his afternoons with Harley. Five Rocks wouldn't be Five Rocks without Harley Jones puttering around, even if he'd stopped doing any real work on the ranch years ago.

"Houseguests?" Harley had reason to look surprised. There hadn't been a houseguest at Five Rocks for years. "Who you got staying at the ranch?"

Gabe mused at his own reluctance to own up to what he'd done. "Tiny pink things." He'd found markers on his study desk this morning. Actually, he'd found marker *drawings* on his study desk blotter, too. A great big pink blob he suspected was supposed to be a heart. Or an elephant. Or a flower—it was tough to tell.

Harley turned toward him, cupping a hand to one ear. "Come again? You got piglets up at the house?"

Now Gabe laughed outright. "Not piglets. Little girls. Two little four-year-old girls and their mother. They're staying with us since Roz Sackett wasn't much for the noise and they need to stay in Haven."

"You took in little girls?" Harley shook his head. "That's a first. No wonder you're knocking on my door so early." Harley got two cups down from his cupboard. "Ain't nowhere for them to stay in town? Really?"

"The Blue Bonnet's full up with some women's thing and we need Avery Culpepper and her girls to be present at the anniversary celebration."

"Culpepper? More kin of Cyrus's, you mean?"

Gabe remembered that Harley's health had forced him to miss the last several Lone Star Cowboy League meetings—the old man knew nothing of the soap opera that had played out in the last few months. "His *real* long lost granddaughter, to be exact."

"I thought you said she showed up last month."

"Yes and no." Gabe reached for a simple way to recount the crazy turn of events. "Turns out that Avery Culpepper wasn't the real Avery Culpepper, but a gold digger out to grab Cyrus's estate."

"No kidding? Sounds just like ol' Cyrus to be stirring up trouble even from his grave." He pointed a bony finger at Gabe. "So you got the real Avery—and her daughters, no less—living with you down at the big house?" Harley began to laugh but it dissolved into a hacking cough that had the old man reaching for his handkerchief and sitting for a spell. "How's that working out?" he snickered in between wheezes.

Gabe felt himself smile. "I'm here before you put the coffee on. What do you think?"

Harley shook his head and dabbed his eyes. "You're a good man, Gabe. A bit crazy from the sound of it, but a good man." He made to rise as the coffeepot boiled, but Gabe stopped and got up himself so that Harley could sit and recover his breath. "The funeral was months ago. Why's she here now and not then?" Harley asked.

"Cyrus made his granddaughter's presence one of the crazy requirements in his will. You remember—we've got to have her here to deed his land and house to the boys ranch. We just found her. The real her, I mean."

"Requirements? There's more than that one?"

Harley must be the only person in Haven unaware of Cyrus Culpepper's wild scheme. Gabe must have told him about the Avery bit, but forgot to mention the other requirement of finding the ranch's original residents. Probably because the hunt for those three old men was making him crazy lately. "Nothing you need to worry about, Harley. We got it covered."

"Good place, the boys ranch." The words sputtered out between raspy hacks that left Harley reaching for his coffee. "You know that. Cyrus knew it, too. What a fool notion to play games with a good cause like that."

"I know. But the boys ranch will lose the best thing to happen to it in years if we don't play along. So we're playing along." Gabe put his hand on Harley's arm, disturbed to feel it tremble under his palm. "Don't you worry about it. I'll take care of it. You know me, I don't ever give up."

Harley looked up. "Never did."

"And I won't now." Gabe checked his watch, not wanting to bother the old man any further with the weight of his problems. "I've got to run by the sheriff's office and pick up some supplies at the store before I get back for lunch. I'll get some oil for that door while I'm out. You take care of yourself and I'll come out in a day or so to fix those hinges."

"Sure." Harley looked lost in thought. The old man really was declining, and way too fast for Gabe's liking.

"Thanks for the coffee. See you later, Harley. I'll see myself out."

"Sure."

Gabe pulled the squeaking door shut behind him. Harley wasn't doing well. Another problem to add to the growing mountain of challenges around him these days.

Avery was sitting on the porch emailing furniture websites to a client—she'd found quite a few ways to keep business going remotely once she put her mind to it—when Gabe pulled up. He hauled a pair of large boxes out of the back of his truck. "What's that?"

"Those," Gabe said with a sheepish smile on his face, "are two boxes of sanity."

Avery laughed as she closed her laptop. She couldn't remember the last time she'd gotten thirty uninterrupted minutes online in the daylight hours— extra adults were indeed a blessing and the sense of accomplishment had lifted her spirits considerably. "Sanity?" She put her hands up to her cheeks in mock surprise. "If only I'd known it came in boxes." Truly, not much in Haven had met the criteria for sanity since her arrival.

Gabe, who laughed, must have felt the same way, for he replied, "Well, if it came in spray bottles, I can think of a few people I'd douse in a heartbeat these days."

Avery walked up to the boxes to see a combination of wood planks, plastic pieces and lengths of rope. Sanity, evidently, came with the label Some Assembly Required. It struck her as a fitting metaphor. "Seriously, what are these?"

Gabe sat back on one hip. "Well, if all goes as planned, these will be swings tomorrow. Some boys from the ranch are coming over to help me put them together so Dinah and Debbie have some swings to play on while they're here."

Gabe was building swings? Was this some sort of incentive to keep them beyond a short stay? Gratitude and suspicion tumbled together in Avery's stomach— she didn't like being indebted to anyone, much less someone like Gabe Everett. And now she'd meet the boys from the ranch. She'd met supporters and volunteers from the ranch—Haven was full of them, as if the whole town had taken up the boys ranch cause. But until now, she'd deftly avoided spending any time with the actual residents. Or on the grounds. She didn't want to know the people whose lives would be directly affected if she didn't stay.

"You don't need to put up swings for us," she blurted out a bit more sharply than she ought to have.

"As a matter of fact, I do. I found markers in my study, and a pink blob colored on my desk blotter. Marlene suggested that if I wanted to avoid my house being overrun with tiny pinkness, we needed some outside playthings." He pushed the boxes up against the trunk of an expansive tree and started walking toward the house. "I've discovered I have a low tolerance for tiny pinkness."

His voice held the not-quite-disguised hint of irritation, making Avery think the "box of sanity" metaphor wasn't all fiction. Which, of course, only made everything worse.

As if to prove Gabe's point, Debbie and Dinah came barreling through the doors with Marlene behind them. "Mr. Boots!" they shouted, entirely too excited to see their host.

"We're getting octopus for lunch," Debbie proclaimed with a ridiculous air of authority.

Both Gabe and Avery looked up at Marlene for an explanation. Preschoolers didn't eat octopus. She certainly didn't, either.

Evidently Gabe did. "You're feeding the girls calamari?" Avery was glad to hear the same shock in his voice that currently iced her stomach.

That made Marlene laugh. "Of course not. I'd never think of such a thing."

"Hot dogs," Dinah said, looking as if she couldn't fathom why the grown-ups weren't catching on. A "box of sanity" was starting to look like a very good thing indeed.

Marlene planted her hands on her hips. "Land sakes, child, didn't your mama ever make you hot-dog octopuses growing up?"

The prickly ball of "I didn't have that kind of childhood" that usually stayed sleeping deep under Avery's ribs woke itself up. Foster homes weren't full of warm fuzzy childhood memories. The urge to mutter "I didn't have a mama like that—I didn't have a mama *at all*" crawled to the surface with startling strength. Avery took a breath, swallowed hard and answered with a simple "No."

"Me, neither." Gabe didn't sound eager for the new experience, either, despite the girls' delighted faces.

"Well, then, lunch ought to be a barrel of fun." Marlene clapped her hands together and headed back into the house for whatever preparations hot-dog octopuses required. Avery couldn't imagine what those might be.

"Watcha got?" Dinah said to Gabe, her eyes on the big boxes under the tree.

"A surprise for you and your sister," Gabe said. He started up the ranch porch stairs, clearly thinking that would settle the matter until after lunch, but he had no idea how wrong he was. At the mention of the word *surprise*, both girls launched on him with pokes and grabs and questions. Debbie grabbed his hand and practically dragged him over to the boxes.

At the mention of the word *swings*, the girls were all over him with squeals and hugs and even one squishy kiss on his elbow. It would have been totally charming if Gabe hadn't been turning shades of red and looking as if he'd contracted the adult version of "cooties."

Trying not to laugh at Gabriel Everett draped in tiny pinkness, Avery said, "What do you say, girls?"

A chorus of thank-yous erupted, complete with one girl clutching each of Gabe's pant legs so tightly he couldn't even walk. He stood there, enduring the outburst, with a face that was mostly long-suffering but not without a tiny sliver of amusement. "I hope it's nice to be appreciated," she offered.

He opened his mouth to say something, then simply shut it again, adjusting his hat, which had come askew in the assault of happiness.

"How about we go help Mrs. Frank with lunch and let Mr. Everett get some peace and quiet to settle in before we eat? I want to see these octopuses before I let you eat them."

Dinah giggled. "They're really hot dogs," she whispered.

"I sure hope so," Gabe said as he tenderly, but firmly, peeled each girl from his legs.

"Swings, Mama," Debbie said with wide eyes as she gleefully peered into the box.

"I like swings," Dinah agreed.

The happiness on the two girls' faces caused a giant lump to form in Avery's throat. Danny had always said he would put up swings but never did. Now, someone she barely knew was erecting swings just for Debbie and Dinah. Yes, it might be to gain her cooperation, but the weight of the gesture still touched her. *I'll buy the swings from him when we leave*, she promised herself. *I'll pay someone to put them up in our backyard. Little girls ought to have swings.*

Chapter Five

Saturday morning, Avery stared at the group of boys who had gathered on Gabe's front lawn to help put up the swings.

It was hard enough to see all those people gathered to do something just for her girls, but the boys themselves tugged at her heart in exactly the way she feared. It bothered her how she could see right into their hearts. That "I'm unwanted" look that lurked behind the eyes of every child in foster care, even on their happiest of days. Could other people see it? Or just those who, like her, had lived it?

"Morning, ma'am," they said in coached tones, as if boys ranch foreman Flint Rawlings had rehearsed them to greet her with good manners.

"Good morning, boys. These are my daughters, Debbie and Dinah." The girls waved, and the boys waved back, sort of. With a collection of boys between twelve and seventeen—near as she could guess—just a shuffle and a grunt was almost too much to hope for.

"Are you building our swings?" Dinah said, squinting up at one tall, lanky teen.

"They are," Flint said, placing a large tool kit down with a thud beside the boxes Gabe had purchased yesterday. "We figured it was the least we could do seeing as to how you've agreed to stay until the celebration."

She hadn't actually agreed. She'd only agreed not to leave *yet*. No one seemed to recognize the distinction. The assumption—and now the swings—made her feel cornered, but she could never quite voice her growing concern. *Maybe you could try just being grateful*, she told herself as she forced a smile in the direction of the makeshift construction crew. *Maybe it won't be so bad to stay and find out what Grandpa Cyrus is up to.*

"I'll be back in two hours to pick 'em up," Flint said as he peered at his watch. "That'll be enough time?"

"I expect so," Gabe replied as he pulled the assembly instructions from the larger of the two boxes. "Five sets of hands ought to be able to get it done in half the time."

Avery settled down on the porch with the girls to watch the spectacle of the slowly rising swing set. She had two sets of paint colors and four other website addresses to send to another client to view products, as well as two estimates to send to potential customers, but it felt wrong not to at least watch since she couldn't hope to help.

Not that the girls didn't want to try. Avery was grateful for the porch rail to keep them corralled away from the sawing of beams and hammering of nails.

One of the older boys stopped and stared at her as

he came back from using the ranch house washroom. "So you're her? The *r-real* her?"

Avery felt—again—the absurd sensation of having been impersonated. No one in Tennessee would ever believe a woman had come to Haven claiming her identity. Quite frankly, no one in Tennessee would think her important enough to warrant an imposter. And they'd be right; if there was any Culpepper fortune in the offing, she had yet to see any sign of it. "The genuine article," she answered the shy teen, who had a bit of a stutter. She tried to laugh off his question, but didn't quite succeed.

"Jake said the fake one was a money hunter, but there wasn't any for her to get, seeing as she wasn't the r-real Avery."

"I suppose so." Avery was of the opinion there wasn't any money for her to get, either, regardless of her genuine pedigree.

"But all you g-got is the house way over on the west side of the new ranch."

"Yes, that old cabin is mine now," she answered.

Even *old cabin* was a bit of an overstatement. In its current state, *shack* was a little bit closer to the truth, but the house had good bones, from what she could see from the outside. Some updating, a lot of large-scale repairs, a vigorous cleaning and a fresh coat of paint could make the place livable, but not for her and the girls. The best she could hope for would be sellable.

"The whole thing's crazy," the boy said, scratching his chin. "It's like one of them m-mystery movies on TV."

"I agree with you there." Wanting to shift the conversation, she looked at the tall, lanky boy with a head of curly brown hair, trying to remember which boy it was Gabe said had the speech impediment. "You're Johnny?"

He nodded. "Yes, ma'am."

"Are you happy living on the ranch?"

"I'll be sorry to leave when I turn eighteen soon." The boy shifted his weight on his long legs. "Dr. Wyatt's been r-real good to me. I ain't always d-deserved it. The ranch is the only place where I ever felt like I had a chance, you know?"

He was trying not to show the depth of emotion he felt for the place, and it pulled at Avery's heart. She knew this would happen if she met the boys—it's why she had resisted it. That hollow place in a heart where it feels like no one cares? She recognized that hole, knew that particular strain of hopelessness.

I don't have to stay to help them out, she reminded herself. *I don't owe these people anything. I get to decide where life goes from here, not Cyrus. Not Danny. Not some scheme.*

None of that was the fault of the boy in front of her. "I'm glad things have worked out for you, Johnny."

"Dr. Wyatt says he'll h-help me go to vet school. I'll live with him and Miss Carolina."

Sometimes, all you need is someone believing in you, Avery thought as she saw optimism fill Johnny's features. She couldn't argue that the ranch did that. *It would have been nice if I'd had the chance for Grandpa Cyrus to believe in me.* She knew that wasn't exactly fair—Cyrus had evidently looked for her, although it didn't feel like he had tried very hard since the anniversary committee found her in a handful of months—but

hearts didn't always play fair. These days, still smarting
from all the wounds of Danny's abandonment, Avery
had begun to wonder if she'd married Danny just because he was the first person to show her even glimpses
of affection, rather than having been the best man to
share her life. *Some day my girls will grow up with
a daddy who treasures them.* If her prayers were answered, it wouldn't matter that the man wasn't their
father.

"Sounds like you're moving toward a fine future,
Johnny."

Debbie looked up from the plastic craft beads
Avery had laid out on the porch table for the girls
to make bracelets as they watched. "Are the swings
done? It's taking *forever.*"

Avery was glad Johnny laughed. "I figure we're
about halfway d-done." He hunched down to Debbie's height. "Fine swings, though. I think they'll be
worth the long wait."

"Okay, I'll wait." Debbie said it as if the wait would
stretch a thousand years.

"You do that." With a smile that lit up his features,
the boy adjusted his hat and returned to the work crew
just as Gabe was coming up the porch steps.

"You met Johnny Drake," he said, looking toward
the young man as he settled into work again.

"Sounds like he has quite a story," she offered.

"He's one of our better successes over at the ranch.
Not that it's been a smooth ride for him. A while back
lots of people were ready to think the worst of him.
Wyatt's pretty much turned him around—and turned
him into a vet, I think." Gabe took off his work gloves
and whacked them against his jeans, sending sawdust

floating into the air. "We don't always get happy endings like that."

Avery thought of the dozens of unhappy endings she'd seen in the foster homes where she'd stayed. "I expect you get more of them than some other places."

"Flint Rawlings? The man who dropped them off? He's a big part of the reason why. And Bea Brewster— she's been running the place for over twenty years. And a whole mess of house parents. And volunteers."

"And half of Haven, it sounds like."

He smiled. "I suppose that's true. Might even be closer to all of Haven."

And there it was: the constant, subtle reminder that all this good work was riding on her shoulders. Well, hers and a bunch of old men who now had to be collected for reasons no one had quite figured out. Cyrus had boxed her in but good, and she didn't much care for the feeling.

"Is that why you brought these boys out here to build the swings?" That came out a little sharper than she would have liked, but she had good reasons to question his motives, didn't she?

"The swings are mostly for my sanity, like I said."

"You didn't bring them out here so I could meet them?"

"Well, now, I won't say I didn't consider it might be good for you to meet them," Gabe admitted. "Mutually beneficial, so to speak. I needed it done and they needed something to do. But mostly, I'm just quickly ensuring your girls have something better to do than finding my study or my library or any of the other places they'd be better off not finding."

He didn't mention the lamp Dinah had knocked over and broken yesterday, but he didn't have to.

"Well, it seems an awfully long way to go for sanity. Especially on a temporary basis." Again, she probably should have left off that last remark, but it bothered her how easily everyone seemed to think she'd become enamored of Haven and never leave.

"That depends. I value my sanity very highly."

"I think you valued your peace and quiet very highly, too." She placed an emphasis on the past tense. "Don't think I don't know how badly we've put you out."

"Maybe, but then there are hot-dog octopuses. Kind of balances out."

It does not, Avery thought, raising one suspicious eyebrow rather than voicing the words.

"I love hot-dog octopuses," Dinah chimed in. "We should make some for those boys."

"I don't think Mr. Everett would ever live it down if we did that," Avery said, watching the horror on Gabe's face at the suggestion. "Let's just keep that our special meal. But I think we could muster up some cookies and lemonade if we asked Mrs. Marlene nicely and helped, don't you think?"

The girls squealed their approval—unfortunately scattering beads all over the porch in the process. Peace and quiet indeed.

"I like that idea much better," Gabe agreed.

As the swings were nearing completion, Gabe walked up to where Avery was sitting going through big books of fabric swatches on the porch steps. The girls were playing some beanbag game Jethro had set up for them in one corner of the porch. "So now you met the boys. Some of 'em, at least. You should go see the ranch."

She looked up at him as she aside set the book. "You really are the persistent sort."

Gabe settled himself on the top stair across from her. "Good work gets done over there. It deserves to be expanded."

"So maybe Grandpa Cyrus got his motives right. As for his methods…"

Gabe shook his head. "Yeah, well, I can't say much for those." He looked at Avery. "Your grandpa was a grouch in life. I suppose it shouldn't surprise me he found a grouchy way to pass." He cringed as he heard his own words. He hadn't slept well the last few days—the new noise all over the house was shaving the edges off his patience. Gabe valued his silence, and that was in desperately short supply right now. "That was a lousy thing to say. I'm sorry."

She gave him a thin smile. "Oh, no, you're absolutely right." Shrugging, she added, "I had this picture of Grandpa—a daydream, I suppose—of the friendly, happy old man who would come and save me. Take me on trips, read me stories, take me out for ice cream—" she motioned out to the construction taking place in the yard "—push me on the swings…the whole perfect grandpa package. Because of my dad and then my own lack of family, I built him up into this perfect antidote to everything wrong in my life. And then I watched as nothing happened. And no one came. And I got sadder and angrier." She hugged her knees. "You can say anything you want about Grandpa Cyrus and it won't bother me. I expect I'll agree with most of it."

She paused for a dark moment and then added, "He's my least favorite person right now."

Gabe felt a pinch in his chest at all that pain. He hadn't any notion of how difficult it would be for Avery to come here. He'd have thought she'd be curious, even eager, to see her grandfather's ranch. It was clear Avery had lots of baggage where her grandfather was concerned—and rightfully so. He knew a thing or two about baggage like that, so he couldn't judge. As a matter of fact, Gabe couldn't say he wouldn't have been far darker and angrier had he been in her shoes. But if he could just get her on the grounds, show her all the fine work and amazing outcomes the place made possible...

"Least favorite person, huh?" He laughed at her carefully softened choice of words. "Is that a step up from the 'I hate him' of the other night?"

He was glad that made her laugh even a little bit. "Not really. Maybe just a more polite choice of words." Her gaze slanted toward Debbie and Dinah, who were a few yards away. "I'm trying to watch how I phrase things, you know? About Cyrus. About my ex-husband."

Again, Gabe sensed a lot of pain lurking behind that very short list of "things which must be carefully worded." He decided not to respond, but joined her in watching the girls as they played.

He heard Avery suck in a "that's enough of that" breath, and shift her weight. "Girls, come over here please."

The way Gabe was raised, a request like that—and now that he thought about it, it would never have been a request but always a command—would have been met with an immediate and often nervous "yes, sir." Gabe's stepfathers hadn't been affectionate men. It bothered him that he couldn't remember how his mother would have worded it. It bothered him that he couldn't call up the sound of her voice anymore, only the weary set of her eyes.

He found himself drawn by the way the girls reacted. Their eyes lit up, they dropped what they were doing and skipped—*skipped*, really, when was the last time he saw anyone skip?—over to stand next to their mother. There was something effortlessly joyous about it that fascinated him in a way he couldn't explain.

"Girls," Avery said as she smoothed out each girl's set of braids, "let's say thank you to Mr. Boots and the boys for building your swings, okay?"

Dinah looked out at the nearly finished construction. "Are they done *yet*?"

The girls were very much alike in many ways, but even he could already see their distinct personalities. Dinah was the thinker, the analyzer, while Debbie was the feeler, the instigator. That insight alone stumped him, because he didn't think of himself as a particularly perceptive man. Cattle, balance sheets, logistics, yes. People and personalities? Not so much. Children? Not at all. And yet these girls intrigued him on some level—not that he'd ever admit that.

"We can still thank them," Avery explained. "So let's start right now. What do you want to say to our host?"

Almost in unison, the girls straightened themselves up and recited a very perfunctory "Thank you, Mr. Boots."

As heartfelt praises went, it wasn't much, but he couldn't deny it had an adorable charm. Gabe surprised himself by extending a hand. "You're welcome."

Dinah put her tiny hand in his—the sight almost comical with those small pink fingers wrapped in his large tanned hand—and shook it with pint-size importance. Debbie did the same, but added a vigorous shake and wildly happy grin to her gesture. Gabe ended up laughing despite himself.

There was an oddly warm moment where all the irritation dropped and everyone smiled at each other. He hadn't expected that, and it unsettled him enough to push himself up off the steps and back to the construction.

Debbie and Dinah followed him like a pair of puppies, skipping up to the pack of working boys with Avery trailing behind them. The girls went through the same routine with each of the boys, offering thank-yous and tiny handshakes to all of them.

He expected the usual grunts and nods, but the boys seemed as charmed as he had been. They laughed and smiled in response to the gratitude. Two of them tipped their hats, earning a fresh ripple of giggles from Debbie. Two of them invited the girls out to the ranch to see the baby goats—something that made them squeal with delight and turn back to their mother with a chorus of "Please, Mama, can we?"

Gabe began to think the impulse buy of the swings—actually more of a desperate act than an indulgent impulse, if he was honest—wasn't such a mistake after all. He hoped Avery wouldn't be able to refuse the boys' offer given the girls' enthusiasm.

"Did you plan that?" Avery said as she came up beside him.

Gabe was glad he could honestly say "No."

"Well," she reflected after a long pause and a large sigh, "I suppose we could manage a short tour as a way to say thanks for the swings."

Gabe smiled and offered his hand to her as he had to the girls. "It'd be my pleasure." He tried to convince himself it was an ordinary handshake.

It wasn't. Her hands were soft and a memorable tawny color, so different from his own skin. The backs of her palms held the hint of olive coloring that tinted the twins' cheeks. His calloused fingers took in the smooth texture of her skin, and he noticed the bare place on her other hand when she wrapped his hand in both of hers. The spot where her wedding ring should have been. All those details in the split second the gesture took.

Gabe was in many ways a detail-oriented man, but this was an entirely different "frozen in time" kind of detail that made his stomach twist and his breath catch.

Debbie broke the moment by tugging on Gabe's hand. "Can we have a sandbox next?"

"Deborah!" Avery chided.

Gabe managed a shocked laugh. "The girl's got spunk, I'll give her that."

"Apologize for that this instant," Avery said in "you're in trouble" tones, accompanied by a very demanding hand on Debbie's shoulder.

Debbie stuffed her hands in her jumper pockets and looked down. "I'm sorry I asked for a sandbox." Debbie did not sound very sorry. Instead of annoying Gabe, this made him like the spunky little girl all the more.

"No sandbox," he said, keeping the humor out of his voice in order to match Avery's disdain. "But I think the baby goats will make up for it."

"We get to see the baby goats!" Debbie squealed. He'd owned pigs and not heard so much squealing as he had today. "Can we ride any ponies?"

"Enough!" Avery replied, her color high with embarrassment and her eyes pleading for forgiveness. "Go on back to the porch now with your sister."

"I don't know where she gets it," Avery said, raising her hand to her forehead with an exasperated sigh.

He'd seen Avery stand up to Roz Sackett. Gabe had a crystal clear idea of where Debbie got her spunk.

Not that he was going to say. Every cowboy in Texas knew not to call the bull out for the size of his horns.

Or, in this case, a mama on the size of her spunk.

Chapter Six

Sunday morning, Avery sighed in relief. Between the four adults, they'd actually managed to get both girls ready on time to attend services at Haven Community Church. Back in Tennessee, she hadn't seen the first ten minutes of a church service in months—they were always horribly late. But at least they were there.

Not that today had been smooth sailing. Dinah had spilled orange juice on her dress, necessitating a last-minute change, which sent Debbie into fits because Debbie always wanted to match her sister. One double dress change and a quick swap of hair bows later, Marlene slid into the front seat of Avery's car while Jethro drove in the truck with Gabe.

"I imagine those men will have a thing or two to say about frilly dresses," Marlene laughed.

"How do you do that?" Avery asked as she checked the girls' seat belts and booster seats in the rearview mirror and turned the ignition.

"Do what?" Marlene asked, her words slightly garbled by the process of applying lipstick in the visor mirror. Avery wondered if she'd remembered to put on any makeup at all in the flurry of preparations.

"Laugh about it all." Did her words sound as weary as they felt?

"Well, I'm not much for the other choice. Better to laugh at it all than wear a sour face all the time." She turned to look at Avery. "A face as pretty as yours needs more smiles. I feel for how you've been slammed down in the middle of this with no warning. I sure can't figure out what the good Lord is up to in all this."

Avery shrugged. "Neither can I."

"Mama, my bow came out," called Dinah.

"Hang on to it and we'll fix it when we get there," Avery advised, giving her own hair a quick check in the mirror.

"You look just fine," Marlene said with a wink, then cast her glance back over to the backseat. "Little girls in Sunday dresses. Is there any sweeter thing?"

"*Quiet* little girls in Sunday dresses?" Avery often felt as if the entire congregation of her church back home barely tolerated her noisy girls. No one ever came out and said anything, but that might be due to the fact that people rarely talked to her at all since Danny left. It had been his church, and had never quite become hers. When she returned, Avery promised herself to find the energy needed to look for another one.

Marlene waved off the comment. "Don't you give a mind to that. We're a family church, and families are noisy. I expect those two will trot off to children's church and make loads of friends. My great-grandkids love to come to Haven because of how much fun the children's activities and Sunday school are. Next year your girls will be old enough to go to Sunday school, and they'll love that, I promise you."

There it was again. Why was everyone in Haven so quick to assume Avery was here to stay? No matter how many times she pointed out the temporary nature of her visit, folks talked as if her permanent residency was a done deal. Avery knew they meant it in a welcoming way, but given her circumstances she couldn't help but feel just the tiniest bit trapped.

"Have you met Pastor Andrew Walsh yet?"

"Only briefly," Avery replied as she followed Gabe's truck around a turn.

"He's a good man. Good-looking and single, too, but not for much longer. Everyone knows Katie Ellis—she's the boys ranch secretary, if you didn't know—won his heart. Bless that man, poor Katie had to wait forever for him to catch on and finally ask her out. That preacher may be wise in the Lord, but he sure was slow on the uptake in the romance department."

Marlene's chuckle made Avery smile. Small towns were pretty much the same everywhere. It was a sure thing Haven hosted a crowd of old-hen matchmakers the same as where she'd come from in Tennessee. She hoped those old wagging tongues wouldn't get any ideas about her—romance was definitely not on the table for her here. And not in Tennessee, either, until she and the girls were on more solid footing. The next man in Debbie's and Dinah's lives was going to stay and dote on them forever.

"Of course, love has had a good run in Haven lately. First there was Tanner and Macy—she has a nephew she's raising who's not much older than your girls." Marlene began ticking couples off on her fingers. "Then Heath and Josie—oh, she just had her darling baby, Joy. Cutest little thing, that girl. After that it was—"

"There's more?"

"Like I said, love has had a good run in Haven these days. Then came Heath's buddy Flint and sweet Lana. Has Lana showed you that photo she found of your grandpa yet? If not, you ask her—you ought to have it. Let's see, Nick and Darcy were next, and then I think it was Dr. Wyatt and Carolina. Carolina's got a little boy a bit younger than your girls."

Avery began to wonder if Pastor Andrew knew he ought to be ring shopping, given the town's romantic track record. She tried not to look stunned when it appeared Marlene wasn't yet done. "And... nope, that's all of them. So far, that is. Five couples since October."

"Maybe you ought to advertise," Avery quipped. "Clearly, there's something in the town water supply."

Marlene laughed. "Well, maybe, but I credit our mystery matchmakers for some of it."

"Mystery matchmakers?"

"Someone's been nudging those couples together. Or trying to—there have been as many hits as there have been misses. Notes, dance invitations, why, even pies have shown up in the name of romance around here. Someone—or a group of someones—seems bent on making sure there are no lonely hearts in Haven, Texas. Jethro says this town's a haven for the soul. I say it's just stepping up as a haven for the heart, too."

And a headquarters for crazy bequest schemes,

Avery silently added. If she did give in to the town's insistence that she stay, would she end up in the sights of those overactive matchmakers before all was said and done? Avery didn't much care for that prospect, and chalked it up as another mark in the column of reasons she might be better off leaving.

She pulled her sedan into the parking space to the left of Gabe's truck. Gabe hopped out and opened the door for Marlene, gentleman that he was. Had Danny ever done that for her? To avoid letting that thought sour in her brain, Avery popped out and opened the back door to begin unbuckling the girls.

"Girls, what happened?" Not only was Dinah's bow missing, but both of Debbie's shoes were also nowhere to be found.

"They itched," Debbie offered, wiggling her toes under white tights.

"Shoes cannot itch," Avery explained as she unbuckled the seat belt and began thrusting her hands under the passenger seat until her fingers landed on the shoes. "It was a five-minute ride, Dinah. How did you manage to get both off?"

"It wasn't hard," Dinah replied, sliding off the booster as if walking into church in stocking feet would be fun.

"Sit," Avery commanded, working the patent leather straps through the buckles as quickly as she could. "I was really looking forward to walking into church on time, girls."

"The bell hasn't rung yet," Marlene advised. "In my book, if the bell isn't done ringing, you're on time."

"Is your church fun?" Debbie asked Marlene with as skeptical a look as Avery had ever seen on a four-year-old. Out of the corner of her eye, Avery saw an amused smile erupt on Gabe's face before he could smother it.

"I like to think so," Jethro said as if the question was perfectly natural. Avery loved that about Jethro—no matter what off-the-wall comment or question Dinah or Debbie dreamed up, Jethro spoke to them as if they were real, serious, worthwhile people. *Give me some of that kind of patience*, she prayed as she finished Dinah's buckle. *Slow me down enough to pay that kind of attention*.

"Take a deep breath, we're here," Marlene whispered in Avery's ear as if she'd heard the prayer. "God doesn't much care *how* you show up, just *that* you show up." With that, Marlene extended a hand to Dinah and walked toward the church as calm as could be.

Avery huffed a lock of hair off her forehead as she grabbed her handbag. "She's right," Gabe said. "Nothing too fancy for little ones inside. And when they scurry off to children's church, you get some peace and quiet of your own."

"I could use that," she replied.

"Couldn't we all?" he said with a grin as they started toward the door.

Gabe had never worked so hard to pay attention in church since he was five.

Normally, he liked church, welcomed the grounding it gave him for the often hectic week ahead. Pastor Andrew taught well, giving thoughtful and even challenging sermons, and what the choir often lacked in talent they made up for in enthusiasm.

This morning, it felt like God had hidden Himself behind a mountain of distractions Gabe was helpless to overcome. The girls were all squirms and whispers, dropping things and making noises. Marlene and Jethro flanked them on one side, with Avery and himself on the other, but even one body away the girls invaded his worship and concentration. It embarrassed him how he resented the intrusion—he shouldn't fault the girls for being four any more than he could fault a cow for chewing cud. Still, it seemed as if every corner of his life had been invaded—at his invitation, no less—by "tiny pinkness."

What are You up to, Lord? He prayed as the girls slid themselves off the pew and trotted forward for their children's moment with Pastor Andrew. *You know I'm out of my depth here. I need more calm and order in my life, not less. You've heaped enough on my plate without all this.*

Gabe had never much paid attention to the children's moment in services before, but today he found himself impressed with how Pastor Andrew boiled a gospel truth down into simple nuggets a little brain could grasp. He went out of his way to include Dinah and Debbie in the little knot of church regulars, talking to them and nodding at their answers to his questions. The girls smiled and nodded right back, even giving excited little waves and not-so-silently mouthed, "Bye, Mom" to Avery as they walked past her with the volunteer on their way to children's church.

The church always felt a little more settled when the young ones left, but today Gabe felt as if his entire pew exhaled in relief as the girls departed. He felt Avery practically slump back in her seat, newly aware of the tension she must have felt. Had he truly realized the scrutiny she must feel? If he felt as if the whole town was watching him fail to turn up Theodore Linley, how must she feel with all of Haven's boys ranch supporters hanging on for word of her decision to stay? *I've thought of her in all the wrong ways, Lord*, he confessed. *I've treated her like an asset to be managed, someone with something I need. Now I see what she needs: compassion. Only I'm not so sure I'm the one who can provide it.*

"Now you settle back and let the Spirit do It's thing," Marlene whispered to Avery as the organ started up for a hymn. "If anyone needs a few moments' peace, hon, it's you."

Thank You for Marlene and Jethro, Gabe continued as he opened his hymnal. *I don't know what I'd ever do without them.*

When Avery looked a little lost, Gabe handed her his hymnal already opened to the correct page and pulled another from the little slot in the pew. She looked up at him with kind eyes for the tiny gesture, a version of the look she'd given him over the swings. *She hasn't known much kindness*, he thought. *And don't I know how that wears on a soul.*

Her voice startled him. Avery had a sweet, clear singing voice. He wasn't sure why that was such a surprise—lots of people had pleasant singing voices—except that he'd never heard her use it, even with the girls. He'd have thought someone with that lovely a voice would be singing all the time, especially to her children. Life had certainly stomped too much joy from that woman's spirit. The dark circles that had lurked under her eyes that day back on the boardinghouse porch were only just beginning to leave her features.

As Gabe, Avery and the rest of the congregation finished the second verse, it struck him. Maybe this wasn't all about preventing her from leaving town and forfeiting the bequest. Maybe it was also about taking that abandoned look from her eyes, about wiping that air of desperation away. He only knew *what* she was—Cyrus Culpepper's granddaughter and one of the stipulations in his will. Maybe he ought to take the time to find out *who* she was—what she wanted in life, what obstacles she faced, how all that weight he saw pressing down her shoulders had come to be there.

And if that wasn't a revelation worthy of serious pondering, he didn't know what was.

Chapter Seven

The Lone Star Cowboy League Boys Ranch wasn't everything Avery expected. It was what she expected in terms of appearance—wide fields surrounding a large single-story building with a wide porch, brand-new barn, several outbuildings and the other elements anyone would expect of a ranch property. It was the atmosphere of the place, the warm bustle and happy noise of so many people, that caught her up short.

Without realizing it, she'd pictured it as an institutionalized home for troubled kids. A stern, productive place. The assumption made no sense, given that the estate had until recently been the private home of her grandfather and given how warmly the townspeople talked of the organization. As she walked around the buildings and saw the faces of the boys and the staff, Avery realized it was her grandfather she saw in those stern and unforgiving terms, not the boys ranch. This visit was jumbling up her emotions in ways she wasn't fully prepared to handle.

"This is the learning center we've finally had room to create," Gabe said as the girls ran toward a smaller building off the main house. "The littler ones get stories read to them here, and the bigger ones can check out books and get help with homework. It's a favorite place of lots of the boys—after the kitchen and the barn."

"Books can never compete with cookies," offered a slightly paunchy middle-aged man as he exited the building with a stack of books and some papers.

"They have cookies here?" Debbie asked with obvious hope.

The man leaned down to meet her wide eyes. "The cook, Miss Marnie, makes some of the best around. And she doesn't get too many chances to hand them out to sweet little girls." He extended a hand to Avery. "Fletcher Snowden Phillips. You must be Avery. The real one, that is."

Avery accepted the handshake. She wasn't sure she'd ever get used to being referred to as "the real Avery."

"Pleased to meet you, Mr. Phillips."

"Mama," pleaded Dinah, tugging on Avery's sleeve, "can we go see the kitchen right after we go see the goats?"

"I'd recommend we go visit Miss Marnie first, actually," Gabe advised, meeting with shouts of approval from the girls. "The barn can be a messy place and Miss Marnie may have a few scraps or treats you can bring to feed the goats."

Phillips fell into step with them as they turned toward the house. "You know, Miss Culpepper, I wasn't always a big fan of the boys ranch. I'm ashamed to say I misunderstood the place and even fought against it. I do hope the same won't be said of you, even if your grandpa didn't quite handle things the way we'd all have liked." He shifted his load to the other hand, stopping for a moment to gesture around the property. "This place deserves the chance to succeed. If there's anything I can do to help you help us make that happen, I hope you'll let me." With a nod of farewell, he turned toward the parking lot.

Gabe stared after the older man. "The boys ranch has a lot of turnaround stories to tell, but that one may just about top them all. Was a time we all thought Fletcher would fight the ranch to his dying breath."

That nice old man? "What happened?"

"It's a long story you'd best get from Darcy, but I'll just say he changed a lot once he discovered she was his daughter. Sometimes people just need to know there's someone they belong to, you know? Belonging here is mostly what turns these boys around. That, and a little care and a lot of hard work."

A sensible-looking woman with brown bobbed hair came out of the house's front door to meet them. "I'm delighted to see you here," she said, waving them up onto the porch. "I can't wait to show you what your grandfather's house is doing for these boys already." She looked down at Debbie and Dinah. "And I bet you little ladies don't want to wait to see what Miss Marnie might have for you in the kitchen."

"Avery Culpepper, meet our director, Bea Brewster. She knows everything there is to know about this place."

Bea smiled. "And then some." She pointed down a hallway. "Kitchen's just in there, girls. Follow the yummy smells." The house did smell delicious, with the scent of baking cookies. A lump rose in Avery's throat to be standing in her grandfather's house, where she should have been but never was. She took a moment to stare around the foyer, lost for words.

Bea's voice was tender as she lay a hand on Avery's elbow. "It's a beautiful place. So big for one old man to be rumbling around alone for all those years." Avery found it funny how Bea's words echoed what Marlene had said about Five Rocks. The two women seemed a lot alike to her—friendly and oh-so capable. "We're ever so grateful to be able to put the place to such good use."

One house tour, four cookies, one absurdly crazy and adorable goat-feeding session, and a top-it-all-off pair of pony rides later, Avery stood at a fence with Gabe, the girls between them, watching the horses wander about their pasture. Today she'd felt her heart lose some of the steely bitterness she'd held for this place. No, it hadn't been her home, but it was home to a lot of other people and a lot of good work.

"I'll stay," she said quietly.

Gabe turned to look at her, astonished gratitude lighting his eyes. "You will?"

"Just until the party. Then I have to get back to my life."

"Of course you do."

"I do have a life and job back in Tennessee, you know." She had an urge to keep saying that. "I can only do so much of my work from here and it isn't fair to uproot the girls." Even as she spoke them, the words rang hollow. No one had missed her in Dickson. She'd gotten only three calls from people who weren't decorating clients, and one of them was the preschool wanting to know if the girls should be registered for the coming year. Too much of that was her own doing—isolating herself in the eighteen months since Danny had decided life in Memphis suited him better than his family in Dickson. She should go back with her head held high and try to make Dickson the home it ought to be. At least she had a house and a business back there—one worth fighting to grow. Why on earth would she dabble in the idea that she could start over here, where she had only a run-down shack and where *Culpepper* was a dirty name?

Gabe was finishing up an agenda for the next Lone Star Cowboy League meeting Tuesday morning when Avery pushed open the door to his study and stared at him, wide-eyed.

"Gabe, I'm so sorry." She had on some kooky old hat that must have been Marlene's from years ago, with what seemed to be paper flowers poking out of it in all directions. Her parade-float accessory was alarming enough, but it was her genuinely mortified expression that turned his gut to ice. "I tried to stop them but…"

"Mr. Boots!" a pair of high, giggly voices called from the hallway, giving Gabe an irrational urge to duck under his desk and hide. Whatever was about to burst through his study door, Avery clearly predicted he wouldn't like it. "We have a surprise for you!"

Avery's face took on a helpless apologetic cringe. Gabe held his breath and made plans for a dead bolt on his study door.

Within seconds, two small girls in ridiculous dress-up clothes burst into the room. Debbie and Dinah sported frilly frocks twice their size cinched in at the waist. They also wore enormous wobbly hats with just as shocking a collection of paper flowers piled on top, gloves, pearly beads and bracelets. Debbie carried a handbag twice as big as her head.

Gabe could not form an appropriate greeting to his two guests as they clomped toward him in far-too-big high heels that held their little white sneakers with inches to spare. He could think of no safe or pleasant outcome of this invasion—not with Avery looking like that.

"Hello," they greeted him in unison, giggling the word in singsong, fancy-pants voices.

It was then he noticed Dinah held something behind her back. Debbie fumbled with the clasp on the big handbag and produced a large colored piece of paper. "We've been baking like Miss Marnie at the ranch. And now we're having a tea party," she declared as if it explained everything.

"Good for you," he spit out, his own mortification growing. This was not heading anyplace he wanted to go.

"It's a *thank-you* tea party," Dinah said with great importance. "And you get to come."

Gabe shot his glance up to Avery, who was shrugging and cringing and giving him a "it couldn't be helped" look that was as infuriating as it was charming. *Are you sure about that?* he hoped his gaze conveyed.

"And," Dinah went on, "you're the guesty honor."

"The guest *of* honor," Avery amended, as if that made it any more palatable. "To say thank you for the swings and the pony rides. It was the girls' idea."

That wasn't hard to guess. "And clearly Marlene

helped." Oh, he could just imagine how Marlene took that particular ball and ran with it. A woman who'd launched this granny-housekeeping stint with hot-dog octopuses couldn't be counted on for moderation in anything, much less dress-up tea parties.

"We helped her make gingerbread cookies and she helped us put flowers on our hats," Debbie said as she laid what Gabe assumed was an invitation—folded paper covered in crayon pink hearts and yellow flowers and something he could only assume were tea cups—on his study desk. Someone had doused the girls with a hefty dose of the perfume Avery usually wore. His stomach produced a wiggling sensation at his recognition of the scent, overpowering as it was at the moment.

Gabe was cornered as neatly as if the girls had roped and tied him at the rodeo. They were thanking him—granted, in the worst possible way a busy cowboy could think of—and it would be mean to refuse their gratitude. After all, Avery had consented to stay as long as the anniversary celebration.

As if to test his resolve, Dinah produced what she'd been hiding. It was a dusty old gray top hat—from where, he couldn't hope to guess—with one enormous red flower tentatively stuck lopsidedly to the brim. Gabe fought the urge to gulp.

"This is yours," Dinah explained. "Everybody gets 'em. We're being fancy." She set it on the desk and wiggled her gloved fingers. The unfilled fingertips where her small fingers couldn't yet reach flopped absurdly as she did.

"A well-mannered cowboy knows he takes his hat

off in the presence of ladies," he said, hoping to avoid the inevitable.

"That's not a cowboy hat," Dinah retorted. "You get to wear it specially."

Gabe raised an eyebrow directly at Avery, who was looking far too much like she was about to burst out in laughter. *Oh, no*, he thought as he pushed his keyboard drawer back under the desk. *You do not get to enjoy this. You could have—you should have—prevented this.*

"Those had better be the best gingerbread cookies in the world," he said with the nicest tone his rising reluctance would allow.

"Oh, they are," Debbie assured him. "They're *splendid.*" She worked hard to get the fancy adjective out. Avery lost her fight to the giggles and he barely avoided chuckling himself.

Gabe scratched his chin as he eyed his new accessory. "So I'm to wear this hat, am I?"

Dinah nodded so vigorously her giant hat tipped down to hide her face until she pushed it back up again.

"Does Mr. Frank have one just as…fancy?"

"Oh, no, he had to go into town for something," Debbie said. *I'm sure he did*, Gabe thought darkly. *Let's hope it wasn't a camera.*

"The party's right now," Dinah said, pointing to some scribbles on the card. "So you hafta come right away."

Gabe stood slowly. Very slowly. "Condemned man going to his death" slowly.

"But with your hat on," Debbie insisted. "You need to put your hat on like all of us."

Avery made a big show of adjusting her hat. She most definitely was enjoying this far too much.

Gabe cleared his throat and reached for the thing. It smelled of the perfume, as well—one of them had sprayed the paper flower. *These had better be the best gingerbread cookies in the whole universe*, he thought to himself as he settled the silly thing on his head.

Debbie and Dinah greeted his new look with enthusiastic, if glove-muffled, applause.

There was nothing for it. The sooner he went, the sooner he got it over with. Gabe walked around his desk and held out an elbow to each of his flouncy escorts. "Well, ladies, I guess it's time for tea."

"You're a good sport," Avery whispered as he and the girls clomped past.

"I'm a dead man. Not one single photo or you're out on the curb by sundown," he whispered back, fully aware he didn't mean it.

"I'd never dream of such a thing," Avery said as she pulled the study door shut. "And I did try to stop them."

"Not very hard," he called over his shoulder. "Not nearly hard enough."

"Gabe Everett? The Gabriel Everett I know?" Rhetta Douglass threw her head back and laughed with one hand on her chest. "What I wouldn't give to see that man at a little girls' tea party." The children had made friends at church activity time and Rhetta had invited them for a playdate at the town library with Carolina and her two-year-old son, Matty. After checking out a stack of books, all three moms were sitting outside the library while the children played together blowing bubbles on the front lawn.

"I kept my word." Avery laughed alongside the woman, remembering the sight of Gabe's tall limbs folded around the small fussy table Marlene had set in the front room. "There are no pictures." She leaned in and lowered her voice. "But he never said I couldn't tell someone. I expect I'll have to swear you both to secrecy now that you know."

"We moms need to stick together. Some days I need someone who understands what it's like to raise double trouble. Someone other than their father, that is. Honestly, I think Deron eggs them on some days." Rhetta sighed.

"I can't fathom how you both manage twins," Carolina said. "Most times Matty's a sweet boy. Then other times…" She shook her head and made a weary sound Avery knew all too well. "How are you finding things over at the Five Rocks?"

"I don't know that I can rightly say. Some days are wonderful, and others make me want to pack up and head for the hills, where no one has ever heard of Cyrus Culpepper."

Rhetta looked at Avery. "You still have no idea what that old fool is up to? Making you wait on some celebration after waiting all those years?"

"Grandpa Cyrus has—*had*—a taste for the dramatic, don't you think?" Avery shrugged. "When I'm feeling generous, I think Gabe is right—Cyrus is just trying to make up for all the years he didn't know me."

"And when you're not feeling so generous?" Carolina asked.

Avery scowled. "I think he's a mean old man who died alone because he manipulated everyone around him and I'm just the last one in line."

"Now you know why everyone believed the other Avery. She acted like a Culpepper." Rhetta shook her head again. "That woman. She ought to be ashamed of herself for how she acted, coming here trying to take what's rightfully yours. She thought she was waltzing into the high life, that's for sure." Smiling, Rhetta handed Avery an envelope. "I'm glad no one gave her this."

"What is it?"

"Lana gave it to me to give to you. It's a photograph of your father and your grandparents."

Avery pulled open the envelope to see an old color snapshot. *Dad.* He looked so young and hopeful—barely a teenager, from the looks of it. Too many of her last memories of Dad in his decline had drowned out the possibility of him youthful and happy. She touched the image.

"Lana found it one afternoon tutoring at the ranch. It's how we started to realize that the first Avery wasn't the real one."

"Well, that and her charming disposition and money-grabbing tactics," Carolina added. "She never looked anything like the family she claimed."

"I guess not." Avery found herself lost in the atmosphere of the photo. The trio looked like a family. Cyrus's hand was on her father's shoulder. Her father—not yet her father but just young and dashing John Culpepper—looked up at his mother. June Culpepper. The grandmother she'd never known—Dad had left home after his mother died, so this photo had to be before that falling-out. Her soured image of these people, the one she carried in her head for years, didn't match the people in the photo. It made her heart ache all the more for everything she'd never had.

"Lana felt you should have it," Rhetta said softly.

"Thank you." Avery touched the photo gingerly, wanting to feel them as real people instead of players in this game she'd been dragged into. "I'd like to keep it, I think."

"Grandparents can be good people—and not just for babysitting. Do the girls know their grandparents from your husband's side?"

"Ex-husband," Avery amended, trying unsuccessfully to keep the bitter edge from her tone. "And no, not very well." She sighed and tucked the photo into her handbag. "Danny was never much of a family man. We lived two hours from his folks and hardly ever saw them. That was fine when it was just us, but when we went from a duo to a quartet overnight…"

"That's a shame," Rhetta said, commiserating. "Those girls are adorable. And they must be loaded with charm if they managed to get Gabe under their thumb." Rhetta jumped up for a minute, waving her hand. "Get down off there, son, you stay away from that fence." She sat down again. "That boy. I ought to buy stock in a first-aid company the way he scrapes himself up."

"The girls adore Gabe. Although, if I'm honest, I have to say I'm not really sure why. He doesn't seem to especially like them."

Rhetta gave Avery a sideways glance. "No offense, but the man might be a bit short on the warm personality from where I sit. All alone up there on that huge ranch—seems to me a man with those looks and all that land is alone because he wants to be, not from a lack of female prospects."

"Certainly not with the way this town seems to match up folks," Carolina remarked.

"Marlene told me about the mystery matchmakers. Did they...?" Avery looked at Carolina.

"They did. Some rather obviously false dance invitations for Wyatt to be my pick at a ladies' choice charity dance," Carolina admitted with a smile.

"Not very original, but effective anyway," Rhetta laughed. "I wouldn't be surprised if our secret cupids matched you off—most likely with Gabe."

"He's been very generous to us, but it's because he needs to be."

"Needs? Darlin', that man didn't need to put you up in his own home," Rhetta replied. "He could have paid to put you up in the next town if he needed to keep you here. You've seen the size of Five Rocks— that man is well off."

Carolina leaned in. "Are you sure something else wasn't going on when he offered to take you in?"

"Nothing is going on." Even as she said the words, Avery knew they weren't entirely true. There was something going on between Gabe and the girls, between Gabe and her. She just didn't trust it or know what it truly was.

"That man put a froufrou top hat on. Trust me, *something* is going on." Rhetta sat back against the bench. "And that doesn't have to be a bad thing, you know. Have you decided you're going to stay in Haven?"

"I've told Gabe I would stay until the anniversary celebration."

Rhetta frowned. "But then you'll go back to Tennessee."

Avery felt her hackles rise. Why did everyone assume she had so little life in Tennessee that it would be effortless to leave everything behind and come here? Leaving was what Danny had done—she wasn't about to do that to the girls. And not only that. "I'm not eager for my girls to grow up in Cyrus's long, cold shadow."

Rhetta crossed her arms. "You've given that man an awful lot of power from the grave. Not that I agree with what Cyrus did—I don't, although I sure am happy to see the boys ranch get a larger spread. It's a whole lot of manipulating nonsense, and you've a right to be annoyed. Only I don't wonder if you're letting the bad outweigh the possibility of a whole lot of good."

"You're forgetting that a lot of people here really like you," Carolina offered. "A whole lot more than that other Avery, that's for sure. They want you to be happy, to feel welcome. Surely, that's worth something. I know you didn't come by it in the nicest of ways, but you've got a place here. The girls, too. If there's nothing keeping you back in Tennessee, don't let everything Cyrus wasn't keep you from everything you could be here."

Avery offered no reply, mostly because she didn't know what to say. She didn't really agree with Carolina, but then again, she couldn't deny she was warming up to Haven—and to Gabe.

Chapter Eight

Avery spied the number on her cell-phone screen two days later and a lump formed in her throat. Danny hardly ever called, and when he did it was never for anything good. He couldn't have possibly heard her thoughts about what it would take for her to move to Haven—but she felt caught in the act just the same. She was glad Debbie and Dinah were helping Marlene make cookies in the kitchen so she could take the call in the privacy of Gabe's library.

"Hello?"

"Where are you?" It would have been nice if Danny's question held a tone of concern, but it rang far too much like an accusation in her ears.

"I'm in Texas, like I told you. The thing with my grandfather's estate."

"You said you'd only be a few days."

Why did he care? She needed his consent to take them out of state, but it wasn't as if he actually missed visits with his girls—she'd stopped trying to convince him to be part of their lives months ago. Danny's concept of fatherhood no longer extended beyond his child support payments, and Avery tried to feel grateful that he was at least dependable with those. "It's become more complicated. I'm going to need to stay here through the twentieth."

"What did the old man leave you anyway?" Avery resented the newly interested tone of his question. Did he hope Cyrus left her enough to live on so she could decline further child support? Knowing Danny, he'd looked up the size of the Culpepper ranch and was salivating over what she might now own. This man bore so little resemblance to the man who'd stolen her heart six years ago.

"So far, one run-down cabin. He left the ranch to a charity in town—well, sort of. There are a lot of strings attached, and that's part of the reason I need to stay here until the twentieth."

"So who's minding *our* house back in Tennessee while you're on your *extended* trip to Texas?" He emphasized the *our* and made it sound like she'd doubled her vacation.

"I paid the son of a client to stop by twice a week and check on things." He paid her alimony and child support, but little expenses like this and others necessitated that she keep up a steady stream of interior decorating jobs to ensure they weren't living paycheck to paycheck. She was responsible with the house. She wrote the check for the mortgage payment every month. She did everything, and did it alone.

"Would you rather I shuttle the girls back and forth while I get things settled here? We've got a place to stay. This isn't costing you extra, if that's what you're worried about." She hated the sharp tone of her words, but some days Danny could raise her hackles so fast.

"In that cabin he left you? Have you got my girls living in some ramshackle old cabin?"

My girls. The words burned in her ears. "No, that place isn't livable. I couldn't even sell it in the state it is now." Avery looked out the library window to see Gabe hauling something out of his truck. "One of the ranchers has let us use a wing of his place."

"His?"

"He and his housekeeper and her husband have been very good to the girls. They're helping us stay because I need to be here on March twentieth to find out what else Cyrus has left me. Like I said, Danny, it's complicated. The girls are fine. I'm fine." She tried not to sound exasperated as she added, "Is there a reason you called?"

"Do I need a reason?"

You never call without a reason. "I need to go soon. The girls are with Marlene baking cookies. Maybe you'd like to say hello?"

It saddened her how she knew that question would cut the call short. "No, don't bother them. I just wanted to know why you hadn't come back yet. Don't you have to be back to register for school?"

Avery was surprised he'd paid that much attention. "Registration starts April first—I've already talked to them about it. We'll be back in more than enough time to get all the paperwork done." Her mind thought ahead to parents' night, teacher conferences, school plays and everything else she would probably not be able to convince Danny to show up to. *But I'll be there. I'll make sure I'm there.*

"Don't you need my permission to keep them out of state like this?"

It bothered her that he was quoting regulations like someone who cared whether his children were nearby. For as often as he saw them—which was next to never—they could live halfway around the world. "I'm not moving here," she said, unsettled by everyone's assumption that she was, and her own tiny curl of curiosity that was starting to expand. How sad was it that she felt more welcome in a place she'd never known than the Tennessee town she'd lived in for six years? "Please don't make this more difficult than it already is. The girls and I are fine, we're sorting things out, and I'll be sure to let you know as soon as we're on our way back."

"You do that." Again, his tone was more of a power display than any show of concern. As she looked out the window, Dinah came running up to Gabe holding a heart-shaped gingersnap in her flour-dusted fingers. He stopped what he was doing and hunched down to Dinah's level to hear whatever she said as she presented him with the cookie. Debbie came right up behind Dinah with a cookie of her own, and Avery watched Gabe take the cookies with great ceremony, as if they were treasures. He smiled and talked with the girls as he bit into one cookie and tucked the other into his shirt pocket the same way he had done the day they moved in.

"Avery?"

She'd forgotten the phone still in her hand. "Sorry, I'm trying to keep an eye on the girls while they're outside."

"You're not with them? They're out there alone?" That was Danny—quick to criticize, but slow to offer help to fix whatever he deemed wrong.

"We're not alone here," Avery replied, the power of those words striking her even as she spoke them a bit harshly. "They went outside to bring cookies to our host, Gabriel Everett. I can see them from the window where I'm standing." Watching Gabe's reluctantly charming way with the girls, she assured him, "We're *fine*, Danny." Some small and bitter corner of her heart wanted to add "not that you care," but she bit back the remark. Danny was still their father, even though things had gone so horribly sour between them. A dead marriage was such a sad and ugly thing. She was grateful the girls were young enough that she had managed to hide most of the ugliness from them. She was also deeply aware of how the girls had taken to Gabe like thirsty deer to water. *They've taken to Jethro and Marlene, too*, she reminded herself. *And to lots of people here. Please, Lord, can't You help me find people like this in Tennessee?*

Danny was talking into her ear, going on about some business victory and his precious new truck. She used to love how he boasted, as if he could rule the world. As if they would have the grandest of lives together.

It all sounded like so much noise now. "I really do need to go, Danny. Is there anything else?"

"No. Just keep me posted."

She wanted to ask why, but chided herself. As she clicked off the call, a startling truth struck her like a physical blow to the chest. Danny and Cyrus were alike. She felt abandoned by both. She'd felt abandoned by nearly everyone. *How on earth do I fix that? How do You fix that, Lord?*

As she stared at Gabe, now sitting on the ground

conversing with the girls and eating the cookie from his pocket, Avery couldn't help but wonder if God might have already begun that healing. Right under her nose in Haven, Texas.

Gabe walked outside Friday morning where the girls were "helping" Jethro fix some of Marlene's flower boxes. They had on small denim overalls, and even he had to admit they were adorable. Avery had done up each girl's hair in a set of bobbing pigtails topped with pink-and-blue bows—frilly compared to the overalls, but somehow cute as buttons nonetheless. *Cute as buttons?* When had he adopted phrases like that?

The day you invited all that tiny pinkness onto your ranch, he answered himself as he walked up to where the girls were tapping nails with little flowered hammers.

"Where'd those come from?"

"Marlene found 'em at the Haven Tractor and Supply. Sweet, ain't they?"

Gabe wasn't sure hammers ever needed to be sweet, but the girls held the pair of them up like trophies. "Mind your fingers, girls. It won't feel so sweet if you miss that nail."

"I know," said Dinah with a pout, holding up one finger with a bright purple bandage. Now even his medicine cabinet had been invaded in girly colors? "Mom had to kiss it three times."

Gabe made a mental note to never do any activity with the girls that might end up with the need to "kiss boo-boos" or any such thing.

Dinah must have caught his sour expression, for she wiggled the finger in question. "It's better now."

"But you should still be careful like Mr. Jethro said," Avery said from behind him. She had on a pair of bib overalls, as well, but they didn't look anything like the girls'. She looked like a slice of down-home sweetness, a bit rustic, a bit tough on the outside, but still 100 percent curvy female. The sight grabbed a hold of him in a way he wasn't quite sure how to swallow. She smiled and shrugged, probably thinking he found the overalls amusing or silly, and the warmth of her grin slid under his skin in a very precarious way.

He coughed, scratched his chin and moved to the business at hand. "Avery, the Lone Star Cowboy League is meeting here this afternoon. I was thinking you might want to attend, if Jethro and Marlene can see to the girls for an hour or two."

"The league meeting?" Avery asked. "Me?"

"I figure you're mixed up in all of this, you might as well attend."

"Am I allowed?"

"Seeing as I am the president, I can invite any guest I see fit. I see no reason why you can't come and offer your views. Or at least get a better sense of what all this is about."

"Mom's meeting cowboys?" Dinah asked, clearly impressed.

"You've met a cowboy. You've met me." He tipped his hat, the gesture casting his memory back to the silly top hat he'd endured at that insufferable tea party.

Dinah laughed, something Gabe rather took issue with—was it so hard to think of him, a rancher and the president of the Lone Star Cowboy League, as a cowboy? "You're different," she said through her giggles. "You're Mr. Boots."

He widened his stance, only half joking. "And Mr. Boots is not a cowboy? These are *cowboy* boots, mind you." Gabe was glad to see the question stump the girls.

"Of course Mr. Boots is a cowboy," Avery added. "And a very fine one at that. Isn't he, girls?"

"S'pose," Dinah added with a suspicious eye.

"S'pose nothin'," Jethro said. "Why, Gabe here is one of the finest ranchers and cowboys I've ever known."

"I'll be glad to attend," Avery agreed. She tucked a thumb under one of the overall straps. "But I think I'll change into something a bit more meeting-like."

"It's casual," Gabe offered. Something about the way Avery dressed had caught his eye from the first. Sure, the activities of motherhood often meant she had smears and stains, but her clothes had an intriguing sense of style. She always looked just a bit different than the other women of Haven, but he couldn't put his finger on why. Was that a Tennessee thing? Or an Avery thing?

It shouldn't be a Gabe thing. The warning felt futile. Already he'd caught himself staring at Avery too many times. And now he was munching cookies with little girls when he ought to be checking on livestock. Or tending to this afternoon's league agenda. Or any number of tasks that had gone undone since Avery and the girls had begun to invade his days. *Things are slipping out of your grasp, and that's not good. Folks are depending on you, and Theodore Linley is still nowhere to be found. Mind you, don't get distracted by what shouldn't ever be yours.*

"I've got some errands to attend to, but I'll be back in time to welcome everyone for the three-o'clock meeting. That gives you four more than enough time to finish—" he waved his hands at the collection of dainty hammers, nails, benches and distracting females in overalls "—whatever it is y'all were doing."

"Fixing," Dinah proclaimed.

"Maybe we'll just have to use the league meeting as an excuse for me and the missus to take you girls into town for pie at Lila's Café."

"Pie!" shouted the girls.

"Can we, Mama?" Debbie asked.

Avery sighed. "It'll spoil your supper for sure, but I don't see how I can say no to an offer like that." She leaned down and tugged on Debbie's pigtail, affection washing over her features in a way that made Gabe's stomach do a flip. "I sure hope somebody remembers to bring me back a slice."

"I will, Mama," Dinah said. "You like cherry."

"That I do," Avery said, straightening up.

"Lila makes good cherry pie," Gabe offered, feeling foolish for the heat he felt rising up his spine. He stopped just short of saying "I'll take you there some time."

Once the meeting started, Gabe questioned the wisdom of having Avery there. It wasn't her behavior— she was friendly and offered up so many good ideas for the anniversary party decorations that she ended up not only on the party committee, but she also got an invitation from Bea to come out to the ranch again and give decor advice. No, his doubts stemmed from how he couldn't stop looking at her. His brain kept overlaying the down-home girl in the overalls with the stylishly dressed woman spouting bright ideas across the table from him.

She fit in. Not just surprisingly, but effortlessly. As if she belonged here. Which made sense—she did belong here. She was a Culpepper and would own the cabin at the far end of the Triple C Ranch when this whole nonsense was finished.

No, it was the sense that she belonged right here. Debbie and Dinah belonged swinging under his tree out front, Avery belonged sitting on his porch watching the sun go down—a whole host of unreasonable images kept crowding his brain. Gabe had never seen himself as a family man. He was a leader, but he was also a loner. Relationships—the up-close and familial kind—never came easily to him. The few women he'd dated more than once or twice always ended up accusing him of emotional distance, and he couldn't say they were wrong. Children needed to be held close, and life had taught Gabe to keep folks at a comfortable distance.

Now, a trio of females was getting in too close, invading his thoughts. Avery was a woman who'd been abandoned not once, but twice by the men in her life—three times if you counted John's death. The men who ought to hold her close had mostly dismissed if not outright ignored her. She deserved a man who would dote on her, who would lavish her with attention—and that wasn't him, not by a long stretch. That sort of romantic bent had never been his thing.

He could never spout off about how the tawny-colored sweater Avery wore set off a dozen colors in her eyes. Or tell her how the sunlight made her hair gleam. A woman like that ought to hear elegant pronouncements of affection, and all Gabe could tell her was how he constantly thought about how her lips pursed when she was thinking. She'd probably find that odd instead of romantic, and he couldn't blame her one bit.

"So the new barn passed inspection with flying colors," Flint Rawlings reported. "Everything's up and running from after the fire." The burning of the boys ranch's old barn had been quite an ordeal, but some fund-raising by the loyal community and the sharp detective work of Texas Ranger Heath Grayson, who'd apprehended the arsonist, had put the matter behind them.

"I know that was a tough time for Johnny Drake, as well," Tanner offered. "He deserves some affirmation, which is why I'd like us to vote to offer him the scholarship we've been talking about."

"That's the boy who had the apprenticeship with Wyatt, isn't it?" Lena Orwell, the treasurer, asked as she looked up from her notes. "Can Wyatt vouch for the young man after all that running-away business?" The boy had run off in the middle of some earlier acts of sabotage aimed at the ranch. It had been a tense time for everyone.

"Here, Lena, read this. I think it speaks for itself." Gabe passed a letter Wyatt had written to him as president of the league. It was a heartfelt plea for scholarship funds so that the boy could continue his veterinary training. The letter was so compelling

Gabe had already decided he'd write a check for the boy himself if the league somehow found a reason to decline him the scholarship. Someone with such obvious skills as Johnny shouldn't be denied the chance to put them to good use.

"The sign for the new ranch will be ready to unveil at the anniversary celebration," league fund-raising chairperson Katie Ellis said with obvious pleasure. "The sign maker donated half the cost, and I raised the rest in three phone calls." She held up a drawing of a horseshoe-shaped sign that read The Lone Star Cowboy League Boys Ranch, founded 1947.

"That's lovely. We should put it up the minute it's ready," Lena said.

"We should wait until the ranch is officially and irrevocably transferred," Gabe cautioned, keenly feeling the weight of the property's uncertainty. "None of this is set until we locate Theodore."

"But we will, of course," reassured Tanner. Gabe thought that was brave coming from Tanner, seeing as how the man hadn't come up with any hint of Linley's location and the whole matter had landed squarely back in Gabe's lap. Everyone was trying—even the private investigators were trying—but the pressure of finding his own estranged grandfather was starting to mount. Folks said they wanted to help, but it was equally clear they looked to him, as both the living relative and the president of the league, to solve this problem.

Avery caught his eye, and while her gaze wasn't the only one with compassion for his plight, somehow that's how Gabe felt. If it was up to him, Gabe wouldn't mind if he never spoke to Theodore Linley again—and Avery understood that. Yet, for the sake of the boys ranch, he had to leave no stone unturned and find Linley. The thought of that fine ranch being sold to become a strip mall burned in his gut. *Cyrus, you old buzzard*, he thought bitterly. *Why did you have to do this?*

"Is there any other business?" he asked, and the startled looks of the other league members told him his words had been sharper than was necessary.

"I think we're done," Lana said, one eyebrow raised.

"The only other business left is to find Linley," Tanner added. The guy didn't know the weight of his words. *Don't you think I know that?* Gabe wanted to shout. *Don't you think that's keeping me up nights?*

Chapter Nine

The house was so quiet after all the league members left, it was as if the world had temporarily shut down. Avery poured two cups from the coffee Marlene had set out for the meeting and went to find Gabe on the porch. He'd ended the meeting abruptly and sharply—well, more sharply than the usual Gabriel Everett efficiency, that is—and she could see how the whole boys ranch situation weighed on him.

Up until now, she'd only really thought about how the situation weighed on *her*. How so much was riding on her commitment to stay. Today showed her how much Gabe felt Cyrus's absurd demands rested on his shoulders.

He stood at the corner of the house's wide front porch, with shoulders tightly set and spine angrily erect. Like a man holding up the whole world and tiring of the strain.

She cleared her throat and offered the coffee when he turned. Dinah and Debbie were still out on their excursion to Lila's with the Franks, and with a start she realized this was the first time she had ever been alone with Gabe. The realization took her pulse up an irrational notch. "You okay?" she said quietly, even though she already knew the answer.

"I'll get by." His exhale said everything his answer did not.

"The boys ranch is really important to you."

"Yeah…" The single word was soft, as if it pained him to admit his loyalty. "More…well, more than most people know."

Was he hesitating because he didn't want to pressure her into complying, or was there something else behind the answer? Avery came around to rest against the porch rail and face him, so she could see his eyes. If you could see a memory in a gaze, it was clear Gabe had some kind of history with the boys ranch that stretched beyond Haven's collective civic pride.

"It seems like a good cause," she offered. "You know, kids straightened out, lives changed…"

"Mine," he said, shifting his gaze to look right at her. The intensity of his regard almost made her swallow hard—the man had such a powerful presence.

"Yours?"

"I was at the ranch when I was eight. I wasn't exactly a model kid, if you know what I mean. I was angry at my dad for dying, my mom was at her wit's end trying to make ends meet, and my grandfather— that'd be our long lost Theodore—just up and disappeared when Mom was hanging on by a thread. I took it out on the world in every way I could think of. And believe me, I thought of a lot of ways."

She knew what that anger felt like. They had that in common. "Why didn't you tell me that before? When we were visiting the ranch?"

"And make you feel further indebted to the man putting you up in his home? A 'force you to save the ranch that saved me' campaign? I'd like to think I can be persuasive, maybe even persistent, but I don't aim to be manipulative." He took a sip of the coffee. "I think Cyrus has given us enough of a dose of that medicine, don't you?"

Did he realize that the fact he *hadn't* used that information wielded twice as much power to convince her than if he had? For all of Cyrus's backing her into a corner, Gabe had held back to give her as much choice as possible. "I meant what I said. I will stay and meet the requirement." She'd told him that on their first visit to the ranch, but it surprised her how much she truly meant it right now. "And I will help Bea decorate the house—as much as I can while I'm here. You don't have to convince me to help anymore."

But it wasn't just about her help, was it? The final obstacle of Theodore Linley hung so heavily around his shoulders that Gabe looked beaten—something she'd deemed impossible in a man of his size and command. "You'll find your grandfather." It felt like hollow reassurance, but she wanted to say *something*.

"I'll have to. We're running out of time. Only I don't know what else I can do."

The end of one's rope was familiar territory to Avery. "There's always prayer. When I can't think of what else to do, it's the only thing left. I know it's supposed to be our first step instead of a last resort, but I guess I'm still working on that."

Gabe set down the coffee cup on the porch rail and leaned heavily against it with both hands. Again, the vision of him being pressed down by demands struck her with such force. Oh, sure, he seemed to hold himself at a distance from people, but it was clear to her that this man cared a great deal. Maybe even too much. *It'd kill him to fail the ranch*, she thought to herself. And that's just how he'd see it—that *he* failed the ranch. Not the dead man who set impossible demands or the lost grandfather who refused to be found, but him. And she knew, just as clearly, that no one would ever be able to convince him otherwise.

Find Theodore. She felt the prayer seep up with a fervor she'd never have expected. *You know where he is, Lord. Show him to these good people. I've decided to stay and do my part, but what good will that do if they fail on account of Theodore?*

And again, for what felt like the hundredth time, a stab of bitterness rose up in her chest against Cyrus. *Why'd you do this, you mean old man? Why put these people—and me—through this?*

Gabe's voice broke into her thoughts. "If this fails, it won't be your fault, you know." Avery couldn't believe he was attempting to console her when he was in so much clear pain. "No one will blame you if we have to send boys elsewhere and live with a stupid strip mall instead of what we ought to have."

He didn't say it, but it radiated out of him just the same: *They'll blame me.*

"It won't be your fault, either."

Gabe didn't respond, just shifted his weight against the porch rail. She put a hand on his shoulder, wanting somehow to make him see that this wasn't all on him.

The touch was a mistake. It startled both of them. They'd lived in the same house for almost two weeks, and the girls had flung themselves on him countless times, but *they* had never touched. In all honesty, she'd avoided coming close to him, subtly aware of the pull she'd started to feel, the humming connection that now seemed to fill the air between them.

She heard him pull in a breath, felt the muscles work under her hand. She told herself to pull the hand away, but didn't.

"It won't be your fault," she repeated. "It's both of our grandfathers' faults." Her use of the word *our* made the connection go from a hum to a roar. They understood each other. Each of them had a specific family connection to this whole nonsense that no one else in Haven shared.

And that was a dangerous thing to admit at the moment. It was as if that glimmer of attraction that she'd been denying since she had met Gabe suddenly stood up and demanded to be recognized.

Recognized, well, that couldn't be helped at the moment. Acted on? *That* she could control. Avery tried to remove her hand casually, inconspicuously, but it failed to feel anything like that. She couldn't look at Gabe, nor could he look at her, which meant that they both had felt that unwelcome zing that still coursed through her fingertips.

Looking down at her hands—because that was certainly a better place to look than at Gabe—she discovered she was running her thumb across the pads of her still-tingling fingers. She swallowed a large gulp of coffee and stuffed the offending hand in her skirt pocket.

I'm raw, that's all. Not in a good place to interact with the male species. Too many fresh scars. My heart

*is still screaming, "Man equals damage," and until
that's no longer true, I'm a walking target.*

This was a fine insight, to be sure, but not terribly
useful to get her out of the wildly uncomfortable silence that hung gaping between them. "Family," she
said in an awkward half laugh that fooled neither of
them. "What are you gonna do, huh?"

While Gabe seemed to be able to keep up a calm
exterior much better than she could, she did notice
one hand's white-knuckle grip on the porch rail while
he gulped the coffee with the same sense of "I'm hiding in this mug" she felt. At least the coffee gave them
both something to do while she groped for a good
exit line. The girls had always provided an easy out
when things pulled a little too close between them,
but they were in town.

"I think I'll take advantage of the quiet to start
on some of those decorating ideas for the celebration and maybe a sketch or two for that parlor wall."
She'd surprised herself by saying yes not only to party
decorations, but also to coming up with some decor
themes for the new ranch house. It was her family's
property, after all. That first visit had dissolved such
a startling load of bitterness that she actually found
herself looking forward to going back. Who would
have thought?

"Need any help? I've probably got some of the
ranch floor plans around here somewhere."

Help? Gabe Everett did not look like the kind of
guy to lend a hand with decorations. His eyes flashed
a desperate sort of regret—the same flash she'd seen
right after he'd offered to put them up here at Five
Rocks. It made sense; Gabe was usually so deliber-

ate and careful with his words that she guessed his blurting out something he regretted rarely happened.

Of course he didn't *really* want to help. Which gave rise to the second, far more unsettling thought: he just didn't want to be alone. This, from a man who struck her as solitary? He truly was rattled by all this. Couldn't everyone in Haven see that? Or had the similarity of their situations just offered her a clearer view?

He'd opened his home to her. Laid aside the peace and quiet of his home to help her. She couldn't decline, even though every time she looked at him she felt some little piece of her unravel, some little strip of hard scar peel away to expose the raw nerve underneath.

Like an idiot, he'd asked if she needed any help.

What on earth was wrong with him? Decorations were so far out of his wheelhouse he had no business asking that question. "Sorry," he said, backpedaling as he saw the shock in her eyes. "That was stupid. I didn't sleep well last night, and I clearly haven't had enough coffee yet today." Another dumb remark, considering it was four thirty in the afternoon.

"Awake all night worried about today's meeting?"

He wished. "Nightmare, actually. I dreamed Cyrus's strip mall was eating me alive."

"That threat does put a lot of pressure on you."

"No, literally, I dreamed the strip mall was eating me alive. Doors chomping at my boots, parking lot strip lines tangling around my heels, that sort of thing."

"Gruesome," she replied. "The demands are bad

enough, and no one wants to send any boys elsewhere, but to hang the threat of a strip mall instead
of the boys ranch over everybody's heads like that?
Honestly, it's just plain mean." They both clung to
the new subject like a lifeline pulling them out of the
mire of her touching him.

She'd touched him. The girls had climbed all over
him until he felt like a piece of playground equipment
some days, but the tenderness of Avery's touch nearly
knocked him over. He'd been strung so tight since last
night's nightmare. Debbie and Dinah's sweet gesture
of cookies had finally put a chink in that dark gray
wall he felt around him today, and Avery had managed to waltz right through that crack and touch him
just now. He wasn't ready for it, he hadn't put the wall
back up far enough and she'd gotten inside.

Who has he kidding? She'd been getting inside
since that day on the porch. Her with those sweet,
weary eyes and that all-too-rare smile and that stubborn independence.

"Sure, you can help." Her words had what he
guessed was a professional confidence to them, but
her eyes looked as if she was scrambling to come up
with some way he could do the least damage.

Save yourself. "You probably should get a committee of ladies to do that sort of thing, not me."

Oops. One dark eyebrow rose, as if he'd challenged
her without meaning to. "No, I think we can make
it work. I have male clients back in Tennessee. And
this is a boys ranch after all, so its decorative scheme
should be masculine. A man opposed to *tiny pinkness*
is a good place to start."

"I can't do anything like that. I don't even like

parties, and you can see my home is no showplace, despite Marlene's endless efforts."

"All homes—and all events—can start on a basic decorative concept. A *feel*, if you will."

"Parties have *feels*? I know that I *feel* forced into a silly party Cyrus is shoving down my throat."

Avery laughed a little bit and then turned to start walking into the house. Her whole body had changed—spine straight, shoulders back, focused. Not as soft as she had been a moment before, but with a new, intriguing energy. "Well, that's no concept to launch a party on," she called over her shoulder. "Even one that's been shoved down your throat. We'd do better starting with your house. Come on."

He ran his hands through his hair. "Shouldn't you be doing this with Marlene?"

"It's your house—it should reflect you. I'm sure Marlene would agree. All you have to do is show me two things. Get some more coffee and meet me in the kitchen."

Now I've gone and done it. I'm going to be some weird decorating experiment. As if he hadn't already endured far too many new experiences since Avery's arrival. Gabe emptied his mug and headed into the kitchen.

She turned back up just as he was adding cream to his coffee, toting a notebook and the rectangular deck of colored cards bolted together at one end he'd seen her sorting through earlier. "Is this gonna hurt?" he asked.

"You may have to think. Will that hurt?" There was just enough teasing in her voice to let Gabe consider this might be more interesting than awful. He wasn't totally convinced which. He watched her refill her coffee mug, adding a generous amount of cream and sugar.

"Is there a piece of furniture or lamp or something in this house that you hate?"

He hadn't expected that as the first question. "How about we just focus on the party for now?"

"Oh, no, you don't. Come on, humor me."

I sat through a tea party—isn't that enough humoring for one guy? Still, he was a bit curious why she'd asked that question. It didn't take long to come up with a selection.

"That chair in the back of the library. The one with all the fussy flowers on it."

Avery picked up her coffee. "I hadn't noticed. Let's go see."

Noticed? The thing stuck out like a neon sign to him, all prim and proper in the warm woodwork of his library.

Avery studied it with her head cocked to one side. She took a long drink of coffee, then looked back at him and asked, "May I?"

"It's a chair. You're supposed to sit in it."

She settled into the old chair, wincing at the squeaks and groans the piece gave under even her small weight. "You haven't sat in this, I take it?"

Gabe leaned up against the library shelves, watching her "work."

"Pretty sure I'd break it if I did. Not that I'd care."

Avery ran one hand down the worn upholstered arm. The realization that it was the same hand that had touched his shoulder kindled a small glow below his breastbone. "But you haven't thrown it out."

Now she was poking where he wasn't sure he wanted her to go. "It belonged to my mother."

Her eyes lost their analytical glare, softening as she looked at him. "But you hate it."

Gabe reached for the right words to explain it. "She used to say it was the one nice thing she owned. That wasn't a happy thought for her—I think it became a symbol for everything in her life that didn't work out the way she planned. She did a lot of crying in that chair. I suppose I should love it or something, but I don't."

"So you don't exactly hate the chair, you just hate what it stands for."

He wasn't in the mood to be analyzed like that. "I was thinking this was going to be more like 'what's your favorite color?' than dissecting my sorry past. I don't like it as a chair or a symbol, if that's what you're getting at."

"Fair enough. No fuss, useful is better than decorative. I can work with that." She stared at the chair one more time before squaring her shoulders and looking at him. "Okay, now show me something you love."

For some reason, this felt even more invasive than showing her something he didn't like. He made a show of thinking about it, but the truth was he knew almost instantly what he would show her. Only he was pretty sure it wasn't what she'd expect—and perhaps that was part of the allure of showing her.

Nodding toward the back of the house, he led Avery to the mudroom off the back hallway, the entrance where he came in from the fields or the barns. Once there, he pointed to a small shelf with three wooden tool carriers—long, deep rectangular trays with handles that ran from one end to the other. If anything in the house qualified as prized possessions, it was these, despite their "lowly" place in the back mudroom.

He was pleased to see his choice surprised her. She stared at the trio of toolboxes for a moment. "Makes sense," she said, looking up at him after a moment. "Definitely functional. Nothing fussy about these. Tell me why you like them so much."

He'd guessed she would ask for an explanation, but still felt unnerved at telling her. It felt absurdly revealing. He picked up the largest one, the handle warm and weathered in his hand. Could he explain how using these every day grounded him, reminded him of everything he'd overcome to get where he was today? It startled him how much he needed to touch these right now, feeling pressured and unsettled as he had since this whole business with Cyrus had hijacked his life.

Gabe started with the most important fact. "I made these. During my time at the ranch, there was a foreman there, Willy, who made the most amazing things in his wood shop. I wasn't an ideal resident at first, angry as I was for Mom leaving me on the ranch." He stole a glance at Avery before continuing. "I get why she did it now, but I sure didn't then. I felt thrown out, and I made sure the whole world knew it."

"That must have been so hard at your age. How could any eight-year-old understand something so complicated?" She ran a hand over the handle of the smallest box, and again the sight of her touching his things sent Gabe's innards tumbling.

"One day Willy took a bunch of leftover wood—

discards from larger projects—and began putting them together to make a box like this. I watched him, fascinated that he could turn scraps into something useful." Gabe set down the box and picked up the smallest one, the one Avery had just touched. It was rougher than the other two, with mismatched joints and gaps in the bottom. "So Willy taught me to make one. I made a hundred mistakes and had to do things over two and three times, but he stayed at it with me." He put down the small one and picked up the middle one. "And then I made a second one, better and larger than the first. And then a third. All from pieces of wood other projects couldn't use."

Avery's eyes glowed with understanding. There were probably only half a dozen people in the world who knew the story of these boxes, and Gabe discovered he liked Avery being one of them. "What a wise man," she said quietly.

"Willy taught me a powerful lesson without ever saying a word. I was so busy being angry at everything I didn't have. Willy taught me to take what I did have and build it into what I needed." Gabe sighed. "Sure, lots of parts of the boys ranch turned me around, but none of them more than Willy and these boxes."

"Where is Willy now?"

"Oh, he passed on some years back. And I confess I didn't see much of him once I came back here after my stay on the ranch. Harley stepped in where Willy left off. My stepfather wasn't much of an influence, but Harley took a shine to me right away. He was a hand here on the ranch, and if there ever was a man who was a father to me, it's Harley."

"He's sweet. Don't you worry about him out there on that far corner of the ranch all by himself?"

"I do, but he won't come in. I mean, I bring him in for meals now and then and to league meetings when he feels up to them, but Harley keeps to himself. I go to him, but he doesn't come to me. Been that way his whole life, so I doubt it'll ever change. It worked for me, too—escaping to Harley's cabin is probably the reason I survived all the years on this ranch." He settled the trio of boxes back in order on the shelf. "Those weren't happy times. But I took what I had and made it into what I needed, thanks to Willy and Harley."

He reached to snap off the mudroom light, but Avery's hand met his as it found the switch. Again, the contact seemed to course through him like a current. "Thank you," she said. "It means a lot to me that you showed me these."

Gabe swallowed hard, knowing the spot where her palm lay on the back of his hand would still be tingling hours from now. "You asked," he mumbled as he walked out of the darkened room and into the bright hallway. It wasn't wise to linger for a single moment with her in the rose-gold sunset now filling the back of the house.

The whole house, big as it was, couldn't seem to put enough space between him and Avery. The woman had a talent for asking the most unnerving questions. He'd never been so happy to hear Jethro beep the horn and catch the sound of the twins clattering through the front door.

Chapter Ten

Avery stood with Bea and Macy Swanson in the living room of the boys ranch the next day, taking in the mix of decors. Bea had invited her at yesterday's league meeting, and Macy had come along because she was looking for help with her own house. Bea was right—the short notice and mishmash of existing and donated furniture gave the place a jumbled, disjointed look Avery knew she could improve with a few key touches.

When she told them so, Macy's eyes grew wide. "That's just it—my house doesn't feel like it fits together, either."

"Well, there's so much emotion in it, in your case," Bea said tenderly, touching Macy's arm.

"I'm transforming this house from my late brother and his wife—Colby's parents—but I want it to reflect our new life, too. And then I want to do the same thing with our life with Tanner, when we get married and move to his ranch. How can I mix all those different lives and spaces?" Macy had guardianship of her orphaned nephew, Colby, and was engaged to Tanner Barstow.

Avery smiled. This was her favorite kind of decorating challenge. "Well, I won't say it's not a complex task, in both your cases. And I'll come over to your place later, Macy, if you like, but I expect you can adopt what I'm going to suggest here without much trouble." She looked around the big room, her heart again twisting for a moment at what her childhood might have been like running these halls and being settled in large, sun-filled rooms like these instead of the cramped and make-do rooms where she had grown up.

Bea picked up on her hesitation. "I'm so delighted to have your help, Avery. I like the idea that the place will have a touch of you in it."

Avery swallowed hard. "The wall's a nice neutral, so colors and art are the perfect place to start." As Avery walked through the room, she pulled out the deck of paint color samples nearly every decorator used as a way to form palettes.

Fanning through it, she quickly located shades that matched one of the large landscape paintings over the fireplace and the couch upholstery. With a moment's thought, Avery added a third color that blended the first two into a pleasing trio of hues. She held the samples up to Macy and Bea. "If you added pillows in this accent color, the couch would blend in more easily. And you could find fabric for curtains that would have all three colors. That would alter the feel of the room with only two additions."

"Wow. You *are* good at this," Macy admired. She

turned to Bea. "Isn't that armchair someone just donated the same color? We could put that in here, too."

"The one sitting in the back hallway? You're
right—that would work to do the same thing. You're
a natural, Macy."

"This place is so much bigger, but we can't afford
to buy a whole lot of things," Bea said as she scanned
the room with a critical eye.

"But you can make the place feel visually pulled
together, and that can do a lot for the boys' sense
of calm, even if they don't realize it." She turned
to Macy. "If Colby sees visual cues that his parents
are still part of his life in your house, it'll help to
ground him. Even when you move to Tanner's." After
a pause, she added, "He'll feel like all the parts of
him belong, and it will mean a lot to him later, if it
doesn't already now."

Macy offered Avery a gentle look. "You lost both
your parents, didn't you?"

"I lost my mom when I was about Colby's age.
It sent my life into knots, and I think I gave my dad
even more trouble than Colby gave you." Macy had
told Avery that Colby had stayed on the boys ranch
for a few months as he worked through his grief over
losing his parents in an automobile accident.

Bea picked up one of the photographs of "gradu-
ates" they had hoped to hang on one wall—a family
tree of past ranch residents, as it were. "It's so hard
and sad. What turned you around?"

Avery sat down on the couch. "I didn't turn around,
to tell the truth. I stumbled my way through a series of
foster homes, making trouble in every one. I figured
it was better to reject them first, before they could

reject me. Only trouble was, that never gave them an opportunity to love me, either." She looked at Macy and the obvious care in her eyes. Colby's story was sad, but it had a happy ending.

Avery had photos on her wall at home—heart-warming pictures of Danny and her and the girls—that now were only images. And memories, she hoped. "I can't decide if it's a blessing or a curse if the girls might not remember much of Danny. But Colby? He should keep every memory of his parents that he can. And the boys here should see the long line of history and success that went before them. Here's what I had in mind." She gestured to the long wall opposite the fireplace. "If you gathered a collection of picture frames—lots of different kinds and sizes—and paint them all this shade of maroon." She held up one of the paint shades she'd suggested a few minutes ago. "Then, fill them with photos—black-and-white ones would be really stunning—of boys who've lived here. You could even have past residents send photos to you as part of the anniversary celebration."

Bea clasped her hands together at the idea. "That way folks who can't come in for the event can still be part of the celebration."

"You'd need a lot of frames, but if you got the boys to help you paint them it wouldn't be much work at all."

Bea narrowed one eye. "I could make that happen. The boys have a school holiday on Monday. Can you come by and show them what to do?"

Work with the boys? Was she ready to do that?

"Colby and I could come help if you'd like," Macy offered.

Now how could she say no? "You know," she said to Macy, "the same idea would work for photos of you and Tanner, of the three of you, of Colby, of his parents and any other family photos you have."

"It would show Colby all the different ways he has had and will have a family."

"And show our boys the bright futures they could have ahead of them despite how rough they may feel things are now. Oh, Avery, it's a brilliant idea—you'll do it?"

"You can always add more pictures or rotate pictures in and out. Include old photos and new ones—if they're all black-and-white, they'll look timeless. So yes, I'll do it." This was Avery's favorite part of the job. Her gift was to bring not just beauty and functionality to homes, but meaning. Anyone could make something pretty. Avery had always had a knack for making things that touched the deepest part of her clients. It felt so satisfying—reconciling, even—to do that here. Smoothing over, in one small way, the bittersweet journey of her path to this place.

Avery pointed to the fern-colored couch. "We can mix in a few botanical prints in this shade and some of those tin stars I saw in the hallway, too."

"Lana found those at a flea market," Bea said, standing beside Avery. "I'm sure we could get more." She gave Avery a warm hug. "You're a real star yourself, you know that?"

The praise glowed in Avery's heart. "If you ever give tours to donors, the wall could make a powerful statement."

Macy leaned against the blank wall. "I'm sorry you had it so rough growing up. Without folks and all. And then to learn Cyrus had been here all along? I can't imagine."

"It's no fairy tale, I'll grant you that." She sighed. "I won't say I wouldn't bend my grandfather's ear with a few choice words if I had the chance."

"Oh, I almost forgot!" Macy dashed for a bag that sat at the foot of a coffee table. "I was going through a box of books donated to the ranch learning center, and somebody seems to have forgotten that only boys live here." She produced a small stack of picture books. "Princesses, fairies, flowers, crafts and a few horse books that the boys would find too frilly. I thought they'd be perfect for the girls to have." She grinned. "Gabriel's library is beautiful, but I doubt there's much to entice Debbie and Dinah in there."

Avery took the gift with gratitude. "And a good thing they're not enticed to go in there. They've invaded enough of Gabe's house as it is."

Bea leaned in. "Marlene spilled to Marnie about the tea party." A soft laugh lit up the woman's eyes. "I'd have given just about anything to see that."

"Gabe? Our Gabe? At a tea party?" Macy laughed as well when Avery told her about what the girls had done. "I cannot imagine!"

"He was a good sport—well, sort of. I don't think the girls really gave him much choice."

"Those must be some girls you've got there," Bea said. "Not many people can claim they made Gabriel Everett do something he didn't want to do. Maybe the mystery matchmakers can build on that."

Avery scowled. "Marlene, Rhetta and Carolina have all told me about those stunts someone's been pulling to nudge couples together." She held up her hands in warning. "I'm in no market to be nudged. Not to Gabe or anyone else."

"Not even a little bit?" Macy teased. "After all this craziness has died down?"

When he told the story of those toolboxes, Avery was sure she'd seen a side of Gabe that he rarely showed anyone. Like the pictures she'd just described, it was part of his home that touched his heart. A treasure that she lacked. She wasn't succeeding at shielding her heart from such a powerful thing. Avery shook her head, hoping that would dissuade the women from their current train of thought.

"He's a good man," Macy persisted. "A fine leader, from what I've seen. Seems a shame a man like that should stay alone."

Macy was in love and engaged to be married. Her starry eyes saw the whole world through romance-colored glasses. It wasn't Macy's fault that Danny had knocked that hope right out of Avery, and it wasn't coming back any time soon. Gabe was a fine man. But he wasn't big on emotion and kept most people at a carefully controlled distance. He'd even described himself—deliberately, if she had to guess—as "not a family kind of man." If there was one thing she needed from the next man in her life, it was a family kind of man. "I admit, he'll make a fine catch," Avery said, "but some other day and for some other woman."

Gabe was glad to see Nick McGarrett's truck come up his path. Avery had come back from her "decorating session" at the boys ranch with a stack of new books, and her girls were working their way through the pile in a warm patch of sunshine on the porch.

Nick had come to borrow some tools—the perfect excuse for Gabe to hide out in the barn with someone his own size and gender.

Nick got out of the truck, eyeing the festivities on the porch with a welcome disdain. "You weren't kidding, Gabe. You're surrounded."

"They're not so bad," Gabe said, feeling compelled to defend them, even though he couldn't put much enthusiasm into his voice. "Well, most days."

Nick shook his head. "You with little girls. I'd have never seen that one coming."

Gabe adjusted his hat and nodded toward the barn. "I didn't see it coming, believe me. I just figured something had to be done to keep Avery in town and Roz sure wasn't helping. I thought I had enough space here that they wouldn't get in my way."

Nick laughed. "And you thought wrong?"

Gabe remembered the stuffed animal parade that clamored down his hallway yesterday. "Boy, did I think wrong. How big a hole in your fence do you have to fix?" He elected to change the subject as he gathered the tools Nick had requested. That was one of the best things about Haven—folks helped each other out. Gabe liked that Nick never hesitated to ask for a tool or a hand when he needed one. As such, Gabe knew he could always count on a fellow rancher like Nick whenever he himself got in a pinch.

"Far bigger than I'd like. I feel like I just got done fixing the last hole." Sure, Nick was struggling to put his family ranch back on its feet and Gabe's ranch was prospering with funds to spare, but that never came into it. A man could keep his pride and still ask for help in Haven because nobody looked at each other in terms of bank balances.

Nobody, that is, except the imposter Avery. Even Fletcher Snowden Phillips, who once could have rivaled the fake Avery for seeing the world with status-colored glasses, had stopped looking down his nose at everyone. Fletcher had softened since meeting his birth daughter, Darcy—the woman Nick would soon call his wife. It made Gabe wonder how Cyrus might have changed if he had had the chance to meet Avery.

Avery. He was going to have to fix this annoying tendency to keep seeing things in terms of Avery Culpepper.

"I got some extra wire from a job earlier this year. Could you use it?" Gabe asked as he kept filling the crate Nick had pulled from the back of his truck.

"Sure. And if you've got any smaller shovels, I'll borrow them if you don't mind. Corey wants to help me with the fences, and I don't think he can handle any of my bigger ones." Nick and Darcy and Corey had the makings of a nice little family going.

Again the thought sent his mind to the little family currently reading on his front porch. *That's not the same*, he reminded himself. *You've never wanted that sort of thing.*

"Darcy taking to ranch life?" Darcy had come from money and was used to life's finer things. She was pretty much everything the first Avery wasn't: big hearted, brave and not afraid to get her hands dirty.

"Makes me proud. I'm a blessed man." Nick beamed. "I gotta say, this fiancé gig has a lot going for it. Hey, the way folks are hitching up in Haven lately, even you could be next."

"Not likely." Gabe kept his eyes on the tools.

"Mr. Boots!" Dinah's voice came from the barn door. "Do you have any flower seeds?"

"Mr. Boots?" Nick asked, barely containing a laugh.

"Not one word," Gabe growled, trying not to be annoyed that even the sanctity of his barn had now been invaded by tiny pinkness. Couldn't Avery keep them confined to the porch and the yard? He turned toward the little girl dwarfed by the huge barn door. "It's not safe for you to be wandering around in here without your mama."

"But we were reading about flowers and now I want to plant some."

"Did you ask Ms. Marlene? She's the one with the flower boxes."

"She told me to go find you hiding in the barn and ask you myself."

"*Hiding in the barn.* She's got you pegged," Nick teased, walking up to Dinah. "My name's Nick," he said, holding out a hand. "What's yours?"

"Dinah."

"Why do you call Gabe here 'Mr. Boots?'"

"Leave it, McGarrett," Gabe warned in the most pleasant tone he could manage.

Dinah simply smiled. "'Cuz he wears 'em. All the time."

Nick turned to peer back at Gabe with a mock investigative squint. "That he does. How do you like living with *Mr. Boots*?"

Gabe cringed at the emphasis Nick gave the title.

Maybe it was time to take a few of those tools back out of the crate.

"I like him a whole lot," Dinah said, nodding. "He's really nice. One day he even came to our tea…"

"There you are, Dinah girl!" Avery came rushing though the door, clamping a hand over tiny Dinah's startled mouth. "Next time Marlene tells you to go to the barn, come get me first, okay?"

Debbie appeared right behind Avery. "Hi, Mr. Boots. Whatcha doing in the barn?"

"Hiding," Nick suggested in a whisper as he came over to hoist the box Gabe had filled. He stopped in front of the girls as he returned to head toward the barn door. "You must be Debbie."

"Yep."

"How is it living here with Mr. Boots?"

"It's very nice," Avery answered for her. "We're very grateful for his hospitality, aren't we, girls?"

The twins nodded.

"And we're going to leave Mr. Boots to his work in the barn and promise not to bother him anymore today, aren't we?"

"But my seeds…" whined Dinah.

"I'll take a look and bring you some later if I find them," Gabe offered as they left. He wasn't ready to admit to Nick or Avery how much he hid in the barn lately. He used to hide in his study, but the girls somehow always managed to nose their way in there—much like they did to his barn just now. It was starting to feel like there wasn't a private place left on the entire ranch.

"Flower seeds?" Nick snickered, grinning entirely

too much as he came back from loading his truck. "Does Mr. Boots grow flowers now?"

Gabe considered asking for all his tools back. "Mr. Boots grows impatient and frustrated, that's what Mr. Boots grows."

"Hey, aren't impatients a kind of flower? That'd be kind of ironic if you had those, wouldn't it? Maybe I'll go ask Marlene."

Gabe stopped and glowered at Nick. "You don't need to enjoy this quite so much."

"Oh, I disagree." Nick leaned back against the wall, laughing. "I'm enjoying this very much. Corey's put me in my place a time or two, but he's got nothing on those two little girls."

"It's for the boys ranch," Gabe reminded Nick. "Avery has to stay, and she had nowhere else to go. Surely, you can see it's worth the minor inconvenience." Gabe nearly laughed at his own understatement. Avery's and the girls' stay on his ranch was fast becoming a major issue on several levels, not a minor inconvenience. For crying out loud, he had swings in his yard. And drawings of bunnies stuck up on his fridge door with cutesy little magnets. Was it any wonder he preferred the barn these days?

"How's all that estate stuff going?" Nick asked, thankfully taking the cue to change the subject. "You found everybody yet?"

Nick had managed to pick the only subject more painful than tiny pinkness. "Still no Theodore. I had Haverman look over the will again to see if there's a loophole like we had for Carolina Mason standing in for her great uncle Mort."

"Nothing, huh?"

"Either we prove Linley's dead, or we produce him. No other options."

Nick put a hand on Gabe's shoulder. "You'll find him. Or you'll figure something out. You always do."

He did. Gabe was the kind of man everyone counted on to set things right. He prided himself at being thought of that way. *This is gonna knock the pride right out of me, Lord*, Gabe groaned to Heaven as he walked away from the barn. *If that's what You had in mind all along, couldn't You find a way to do it that doesn't hurt all those boys?*

"Hey." Nick stopped walking. "Weren't you going to look for flower seeds?"

"No need to look. I don't have any. I'll swing by the supply store and grab something this afternoon."

"Gabe Everett buying flower seeds." Nick shook his head. "Next thing I know I'll hear about you buying flowers."

Gabe had actually seen some of the first bluebonnets of the season yesterday up on the eastern pastures and thought about—not actually done, mind you, but thought about—bringing some to Avery.

Not that anyone would ever be told a secret like that. Besides, that wouldn't have counted as *buying flowers* so when he gave Nick a decisive "Nope!" it was the truth.

Chapter Eleven

When Heath Grayson opened his door Monday afternoon, Avery recognized the universal countenance of a new father: equal parts wonder and exhaustion. Remembering the haze of days and nights in those first weeks with Debbie and Dinah, Avery had let Marlene talk her in to adding her name to a church sign-up for bringing the new parents supper. Everyone in Haven seemed to be taking a turn, and Marlene had said she already had a huge pot of chili planned, so all Avery had to do was deliver.

"Hey, proud poppa," Avery greeted. "How are you holding up?"

As if to answer the question, baby Joy's cries echoed from behind Heath. "Ranger duty has nothing on diaper duty. I feel like I'm in parenting boot camp."

Avery laughed. "I suppose you are." She pointed to the burp cloth still perched on the Texas Ranger's shoulder.

He pointed to the paint smears not quite gone from Avery's hands and arms. "And you're still purple from this morning's painting session. I heard you and the boys had quite the time of it." Heath ushered her in with a chuckle.

"It's maroon, actually. And it was fun. I'm pretty sure most of the paint ended up on the picture frames, but I can't be certain."

"I'm still trying to make sure most of the diaper ends up on the baby," Heath admitted. "How'd you ever manage this with two of them?"

"I remember thinking I would never sleep again. I'll bring the girls for a shorter visit next time, but I left them with Marlene so I can give you both a shot at peace and quiet."

Josie came out of the kitchen holding a wailing little Joy tucked in a pale yellow blanket. If it was possible, Josie looked even more tired than Heath. "Peace and quiet?" Josie asked. "I forgot what those are."

Avery walked up close to see the tiny weeks-old newborn in Josie's arms. "Little Joy hit her first growth spurt, did she?"

"If you mean did she reach the point where she does nothing but cry and eat for hours on end, then yes, Joy is in a growth spurt." Heath moaned. "Or a whatever spurt. All I know is that I've done more laundry this week than in a month of my bachelor days."

Heath's words could be classified as complaints, but the affection on the man's face was nothing but pure love for his new family. If he wasn't Joy's biological father—Josie had been a pregnant young widow when she and Heath met—he was surely that little girl's daddy in his heart. Avery felt a stab of regret remembering that Danny had looked at her daughters that way once.

"Would you like to hold her?" Josie asked.

"I'd love to. Let me set my things down and wash my hands." She tucked the pot of chili and the pan of corn bread into the Graysons' kitchen and washed up. Coming back out into the living room, Avery took the beautiful little girl in her arms and sat on the couch while Heath and Josie settled across from her.

"Look at those eyes," Avery cooed. "And all that hair!" The baby had the gray eyes of so many newborns, but the full head of red-brown hair seemed to be the gift of her mother.

"She has her mama's hair, that's for sure," Heath said.

"And her mama's lungs, I'm afraid," Josie said with a weary smile. "A champion crier. I thought being a nanny before would make this easy, but…"

"It's a whole new world when it's your own baby, isn't it? Twice as wonderful but three times as much work."

"On half as much sleep." Josie yawned. "You were so kind to offer to come and bring supper."

"Marlene did the cooking, but I was happy to help. No one should have to do this alone." It struck Avery how poignant she found the words. She probably had looked as harried to Gabe when he'd offered his help back on Roz's porch. If Gabe had offered his help that afternoon, surely she could do as much right now. "When's the last time you two sat on your porch alone together and watched the sun go down?"

One look at their faces told Avery it had been quite a while.

Avery stood. "Tell you what—put the baby swing in the kitchen and I'll get supper on while you two get reacquainted on the porch. If I did it with two babies, heating up supper with one ought to be a cinch."

"But you don't have to—" Josie began.

"Sure, I don't have to, but I want to." She had no way of repaying Gabe, but she could "pay it forward" and help out Josie and Heath. It made her feel more human, less like a pawn in Grandpa Cyrus's from-the-grave chess game.

Joy fussed a bit, but settled drowsily beside an adorable small stuffed goat—surely a ranch gift— in the swing. After a few minutes of cooing until the child's eyes closed, Avery made her way around the Graysons' kitchen to prepare the meal. There had been one or two—not many, but a few—women who did this for her and Danny when the twins were first born, and she remembered being so thankful. Opening the fridge for some butter for Marlene's cornbread, she saw a list held to the fridge door with a magnet.

It was the same schedule for the next two weeks she'd seen at church. Supper was arriving via a different member of Haven Community Church each night. She saw Rhetta was on tomorrow night, and several other names she recognized. Of course, Marlene was on tonight's list, but Avery found herself glad to be taking the housekeeper's place. "Go get to know Josie," Marlene had encouraged her. "A new mom always needs another mom to help hold her up."

She'd never known a community as tightly knit as Haven. Sure, Haven had its share of small-town faults—judgmental old hens like Roz Sackett and grumpy, meddling old men like Cyrus—but it had a lot more of what small towns ought to have. Kindness and generosity and connection. It was getting hard to deny the fact that she felt more connected in Haven than she had back in Tennessee. Still, the obstacles to staying—no place to live, uprooting her business, getting Danny's consent to move the children out of state—weren't going away. It still made more sense to head back to Tennessee and redouble her efforts to build a better life there than it did to daydream about a life here.

The oven timer beeped, and Avery walked to the front door to call in the couple for their supper. At first she thought they'd been cuddling on the porch swing, but a closer inspection showed the pair to be fast asleep.

Oh, those sleep-deprived first weeks, she thought to herself. *Let them be, poor things.*

She walked back into the kitchen, covered the cornbread and turned off the oven. Avery turned to grin at Joy's bright gray eyes—the baby was now wide-awake. "Don't you know you're supposed to sleep when they do?" she cooed as she picked up the infant. "Why don't you and I explore the backyard while Mom and Dad nap?"

She scribbled a quick note to put where Josie or Heath would easily see it, and tucked her cell phone in her back pocket. It showed a missed call from Gabe, but she figured she could return that later. Walking into the Graysons' tidy backyard that looked out over the small farm, she spoke in lively tones to the little girl as she patted her tiny back. "Some day soon you'll strew this with toys. And probably make your daddy mad by leaving them out in the rain. And hand your mommy endless stains to try and get out of your pretty pink clothes."

Joy merely made sweet baby sounds and settled against her shoulder. She barely even whimpered when Avery's cell phone went off again in her pocket.

A little quick maneuvering showed her the call was from Gabe. "You'll never guess where I am," she said into the phone.

"I know you're at Heath's cooing over his baby, but you don't want to guess where I am." His voice held none of the amusement hers had. As a matter of fact, she picked up the distinct and frightening sound of Debbie's cries in the background.

Fear shot through her. "What's wrong?"

"Debbie fell off the swings. Jethro is home with Dinah but Marlene and I are on our way to Dr. Delgado. Meet us there. It's three doors down from Lila's."

Oh, no. Dear Lord, watch over my girl, Avery prayed as she rushed back through the house to shake the Graysons awake from their peaceful nap on the porch swing.

"Is Joy okay?" Josie's startled eyes shot wide.

"Joy is fine, but I have to leave."

"We nodded off," Heath said, dragging himself awake. "Everything okay?"

"Debbie fell off the swings. Gabe and Marlene want me to meet them at Dr. Delgado's." She wished she could be calmer, but her pulse was thundering. *Debbie's hurt. Bad.* She could hear it in Gabe's voice. She deposited Joy in Josie's arms and pulled on her jacket. "Supper's in the oven. I've got to go."

"Oh, no. Of course you do. We'll say a prayer for poor Debbie. Let us know how everything turns out, okay?"

Gabe tried to keep his eyes on the road and stay within the speed limit, but both tasks were hard with Debbie's frightened cries right next to him.

"Hold that arm still now, baby girl," Marlene said in softer, calmer tones than he could hope to manage.

"It hurts," Debbie sobbed. "I want Mama."

"She's on her way, darlin'," Gabe reassured her. "She'll be right there at Doc Delgado's."

"I'm rotting!" Debbie cried with new alarm as she moved her hand from where it held her forearm.

"Rotting?" Gabe was almost afraid to ask. Visions of gruesome gashes filled his brain. He was a cool-headed manager, but little-girl emergencies were not exactly his thing.

"I'm turning black like the bananas," Debbie moaned as the tears came harder.

"Oh, sweetheart, you're bruising," Marlene said. "That's your body sending in soldiers to help take care of your arm. It's a good thing, I promise."

Gabe wasn't sure of the accuracy of Marlene's preschool description of the human immune system, but he wasn't about to argue, since the explanation seemed to calm Debbie. He turned the last corner carefully so as not to bump the tender limb. "Here we are. Doc Delgado will have you fixed up in no time."

"I'm scared," Debbie whimpered. "I want Mama."

Avery came out of Dr. Delgado's door, eyes wide with fear. "She's already here," Gabe told her.

"Baby!" Avery cried.

Gabe ducked out of the door and intercepted the panicked Avery. "She'll be okay. It's her arm. She's scared but..."

"Mama!" Debbie burst into further tears.

Avery moved to scoop up her daughter. "Mind the left arm," Marlene warned. "I don't think we want to jostle it."

"It hurts," Debbie whimpered.

"I know baby, I know," Avery said as she nearly ran toward the door. Marlene and Gabe followed fast behind. He was unprepared for how tiny Debbie's injury rattled him. He'd bought the swing set and had it installed. He felt responsible. And hang it all if he wasn't growing fond of all that tiny pinkness around the house. It felt like all of March was spiraling out of his control into places he didn't want to go.

When Dr. Delgado ushered Avery and Debbie into his office, Gabe's stomach twisted until Avery motioned him into the office with her, Marlene right behind. He'd have stayed out in the waiting room if that was her wish—he wasn't their kin, after all—but it would have driven him crazy.

"I've seen you in church. My Martin's not much older than you. Remind me of your name, sweetheart?" Dr. Delgado's calm, quiet voice cut through the panicked chaos of the last few minutes.

"Debbie," the little girl replied as she clutched her arm. Gabe thought she looked so small and pale sitting there on the examination table.

"Well, Debbie, I'm Doc Delgado. Gabe here tells me you took a tumble off some swings."

The words sent stinging little stabs into Gabe's

chest. Avery hadn't given him a "you hurt my baby" look yet, but it was only a matter of time.

"How about you let me take a look at that arm?" Dr. Delgado asked, gently peeling Debbie's other hand off the injured arm. "Look at all those colors," Dr. Delgado said, as if it was a wonder of science rather than the telltale signs of a serious injury. One Gabe had made possible. "Box of sanity," huh? What made him ever think those swings were a good idea?

"I thought I was rotting. Like a banana." Debbie sniffed with a dramatic air. Marlene offered a chuckle, but Avery gave Gabe a questioning look.

"Pretty clever association, if you ask me," Gabe replied. He felt totally out of his depth and achingly guilty at the moment, as he waited for Avery to lash into him for allowing her daughter to fall injured. She looked upset, no doubt about it, but he couldn't work out why there seemed to be so little anger in her features.

"Well, clearly something's up with that arm," Dr. Delgado said. "I'll have to take an X-ray—that's a special kind of picture that will let me see the bones in your arm. I'll even show you when we're done, if you like."

"I wanna see my bones," Debbie said.

Doc went on with a tender examination, keeping Debbie talking. With each question she answered, she seemed to calm further. Gabe was calming down himself—it still startled him how personally he'd taken Debbie's fall. When Avery and Debbie left with Dr. Delgado to go take the X-ray, Gabe felt like slumping against the wall in exhaustion.

He looked up to see Marlene's very direct gaze

leveled straight at him. "Hurts to care, don't it?" He couldn't tell if she was chastising or encouraging him. The fact that it was probably both just unnerved him more.

He pointed in the direction Debbie and Avery had gone. "That's my fault. I put those swings up so they'd stay out of my hair."

Marlene leaned back against the wall cabinets and crossed her arms. "If you recall, Gabriel, I suggested the idea of some outside play equipment. And this is no one's fault—certainly not yours. Now, getting caught for breaking the speed limit twice on the way over here like you did? That would have been your fault. But not this."

He didn't have an answer to that, so Gabe simply glared at her for a moment and then began fiddling with his car keys.

"She'll be all right, Gabriel. Maybe not right away, but in time. You, on the other hand…well, I'm not so sure."

Gabe stared down the hallway. "You're right, Avery's bound to be furious."

Marlene shook her head. "I doubt that, and that's not at all what I meant. Why is it such a fearsome thing to you that you've taken a shine to those little girls? You care about them, and you act as if that was some horrible itch you can't scratch."

A horrible itch he couldn't scratch. Did Marlene have any idea what a perfect picture she'd just painted of the way he felt? He felt it all over—and getting stronger by the minute—with an itch he absolutely should not, could not, scratch. Ever.

The honest truth was that the more he came to care

about Avery and her girls, the less he could ever hope to be part of their lives. They deserved someone who wanted to be a father, who had those warm, fuzzy fatherly tendencies he couldn't hope to possess. Just because he felt a flicker of affection for the girls didn't mean his lifelong preference for privacy, peace and quiet would suddenly evaporate.

And even if he could manage to grow used to the tiny pink brand of chaos, there was a lot of baggage piled up in front of him and Avery: the long line of men who didn't stay around. His father. His grandfather. His first stepfather. His second stepfather. Her grandfather. Her father. The list tightened around his throat like a pair of hands. Those girls and Avery should be doted upon, showered with affection by a man with a strong calling to family life.

That wasn't him.

Even if it had felt as if his heart had left his chest and wrapped around that poor little girl as she wept in the truck seat beside him. The hole that would open up in his house—and his heart—after March 20 felt acres wide, and Gabe didn't know what to do about it. It made him nearly hope Avery would be furious with him for this incident—her anger would be easier to bear than those looks she had given him in the mudroom the other day.

"Ms. Marlene, Mr. Boots," Debbie called from down the hall. "I'm broken." She appeared in the door with a little blue sling and a white plastic splint secured to her arm with pink elastic bandages. Her voice had a "so there" tone about it, as if the injury had been an accomplishment instead of the pile of regret that currently turned in Gabe's stomach.

"A very small break, I'll give you that, and some serious bruising around the wrist. She should come back in two days for me to cast it once the swelling goes down."

"I can have a pink cast," Debbie said, sounding as if it was a privilege.

"I'll take those swings down first thing tomorrow morning," Gabe offered.

Debbie's mouth fell open. "No!"

"Why would you do that?" Avery asked.

Gabe nodded toward the little girl with an "isn't it obvious?" glare.

"Well, you can't go on them until you can hold on with both arms, but that doesn't mean they have to come down," Avery explained half to Gabe and half to Debbie.

Gabe took a breath to reply, but one glance at the expressions of each of the three females in front of him shut his mouth again. To his mind, the swings needed to go, but it was crystal clear he was in the minority at the moment and he was in no mood to argue.

"Let's get everyone home and settled," Marlene suggested. "I'm sure Jethro and Dinah are out of their minds with worry. I'll call them from Gabe's truck while Debbie heads home with her mama."

Chapter Twelve

It was nearly nine thirty at night by the time Avery was able to settle Debbie and Dinah in bed after all the chaos of the accident. The novelty of her current splint and upcoming pink cast had worn off along with the pain medicine, and Debbie was fussy and uncomfortable. Dinah was worried about her sister and needy herself. By the time both girls were finally asleep, Avery felt as if she was more spent and irritable than a dozen Heaths and Josies.

What happened to the lovely afternoon that was supposed to be spent cooing over beautiful new baby Joy?

Marlene and Jethro, bless them, had gone to bed also exhausted from the day. Avery was just about to follow suit when she remembered a quart of peppermint-stick ice cream in the freezer. A big bowl of that with a healthy dose of chocolate sauce sounded like just the balm for her surprisingly stressful day.

There was also one other matter to settle—and that would go better over ice cream, as well. On her way to the kitchen, Avery knocked on the door of Gabe's study, where he'd holed himself up since their return.

He looked up with a cautious startle. Was he expecting a lecture or another crazy tea-party invitation? With an inner smile Avery realized she had yet to knock on Gabe's study door with any news the man would consider "good." Tonight would be a good time to fix that.

"I was just about to eat my stress by way of a big bowl of ice cream. Care to join me?"

He looked shocked. Clearly, that wasn't the statement he was expecting.

"No special hats required, promise."

"Okay," he said with a touch of hesitation. Did he really think she'd ask him to join her for ice cream so she could chew him out? Danny couldn't even seem to embrace the concept of guilt or responsibility, but Gabe seemed to hoard it. He'd been heart stricken over Debbie's fall, and the emotion seemed as foreign as it was endearing on a man of Gabe's bearing.

Gabe kept eyeing her as he pulled a pair of bowls and spoons from the cupboard while she got out the ice cream and sauce.

"I'm not mad," she finally said, unable to stand his "go ahead, yell at me" face. "Frightened, maybe, but not mad."

"You ought to be." Avery felt as if he was going out of his way to keep his distance as he laid the scoop on the counter between them.

"I don't get mad at people for accidents. Deliberate pain? Yes, I get mad. You already know that." Avery didn't see any need to name Danny or Cyrus— Gabe knew how she felt about their manipulations.

She opened the container and began scooping generous portions into the bowls. Today had clearly been a three-scoop kind of day. "But there was nothing deliberate about what happened this afternoon."

"Debbie's hurt."

"Yes, she is. But I'm thankful she wasn't hurt worse. She's a bold and brave little girl—they both are. The way I see it, bangs and bruises—and yes, breaks—come with the territory."

When he didn't reply, Avery put down the scoop and stared straight at Gabe until he met her gaze. "I don't blame you." And then, maybe because her defenses were long past down, she added, "I'm grateful you were there to take such good care of her."

When he still looked as if he was crawling out of his skin with guilt, she pushed one bowl in front of him and walked over to the counter stool next to him. It was a little too close to him, but it felt wrong to go out of her way and scoot it farther toward the edge. She took the bottle of chocolate syrup and doused the pink mounds of ice cream. "This is the part where you just say 'okay' and stop beating yourself up about something that wasn't your fault." She set the bottle in front of him as if to say "your move."

With a rather unsteady glance in her direction, Gabe picked up the bottle, gave his ice cream a flimsy swirl of sauce and choked out, "Okay."

She eyed his bowl and hers. "Really? That's the best you can do after a day like today? You men and your sensible compartmentalization slay me."

It had been a long day. She didn't want to feel the slightest bit guilty for her indulgence. The words might have a bit more edge than they ought to have had.

With a defiant look, Gabe picked the bottle back up and squeezed a small ocean of chocolate sauce on his portion.

If he'd meant to outsauce her, he had. She laughed loudly, clamping her hand to her mouth for making too much noise and possibly waking the girls. The laugh settled into a stifled, refreshing giggle that seemed to shave all the sharp ends off the day. Avery sighed, digging her spoon in and heaving up a blissful mouthful of cold sweetness. "See now?" she mumbled in ice-cream-garbled words. "Marvelous."

"I don't see how a thousand calories of sugar solves any problems," Gabe said as he systematically assembled a spoonful of equal portions ice cream and sauce. Did the man ever stop managing circumstances?

"That's because you're a guy. Believe me, this helps. Your mentioning the calorie count, however, does not."

"I am sorry it happened. Am I allowed to say that?"

The true concern on his face touched her. Today had shown her his care for Debbie and Dinah in ways she could no longer hold at a distance. Gabe Everett wasn't staying inside the neat, controllable borders she'd drawn around him and their relationship. Ever since he'd shown her the toolboxes—and the glimpse of his heart he'd been unable to hide while doing so— Avery felt her own heart venturing into very scary territory. She could not risk any more hurt—for her or the girls.

"Yes," she replied, frightened that the tone of her single word said a lot more than was wise.

"Will she be okay, you think?" Again, the words

were full of care. Affection, even. It made Avery think, *She might, but will I?*

"Yes," she said in something too close to a whisper, keeping her eyes on the ice cream. Every inch of her felt flushed and tingly. She ate another huge bite so she wouldn't have to speak more.

Gabe cleared his throat. "I know I'm gruff with them most of the time, and they are all kinds of noisy, but... I have to say they've..." He coughed again, making distracted circles with his spoon in the ice cream. "Well, the little pink things have grown on me."

Avery's chest held a fluttery, bursting sensation as if her heart was attempting an escape. She found the notion entirely too accurate.

Once he had spoken the first words, it seemed as if Gabe needed to spit them all out before he came to his senses. "They steal my time, they invade my study, they run down my hallways and yet I went crazy thinking about Debbie being hurt, and on my watch besides. And still, I know the minute she can, Debbie will be right back out on that swing fixing to break the other arm." He looked up at Avery as though she was a puzzle to solve. "How do you do it?"

Explain parenthood to a bachelor cowboy? She could gather every word in Texas and still not have enough. "You just...do." The inadequate reply spilled a tender-hearted laugh from her. That, and a feeling of sympathy that made her heart's escape not only likely, but also impossible to stop.

Gabe was trying so hard not to care.

He was failing at it, and in a way that stole her

heart no matter what she deemed best for her or the girls.

Have mercy, Lord, she wailed silently to Heaven as she looked away from his perplexed and resigned expression. *You take away the man who couldn't care enough only to give me the care of a man who's told me he doesn't want a family? You know we can't stay. You know the girls need someone who'll be over the moon for them. You know I'm raw and wounded from Danny's discarding of me. I can't trust what Gabe is stirring up in me.*

Gabe evidently misunderstood her evasion. "Please don't leave on account of what's happened. I'm trying to find Theodore—and I will, I have to—so I need you to stay."

It was the "I need you" that got to her. She could convince herself he was pleading for something other than the fulfillment of Cyrus's demands. Gabe's eyes had a way of clouding her thinking.

"Gabe…" Avery found she couldn't finish the sentence. She could feel herself falling, feel herself inventing reasons to stay close to this man when she should be planning her exit. She'd convinced herself, just now, that Gabe was as fond of her as he was of her daughters.

He shook his head, shoulders hunching over as if he'd just reprimanded himself. "I know. I know it's asking a lot."

He didn't realize that if he stood up and took her in his arms right this minute, she'd melt against him faster than the ice cream. She'd lay down the steel-willed determination that was her armor in this one-woman battle. She'd let him into her life and the girls' lives even though she knew better.

And what would happen then? Danny could withhold his permission to let her move the girls here. Cyrus's scheme could still backfire, leaving her only a broken-down cabin, leaving the boys ranch scaled back down and removing residents, and leaving Haven with the punishment of a strip mall the whole town would hate. How could she possibly stay and raise a family in the shadow of that?

Staring into his questioning gaze, Avery tried to stop herself from wondering, *What if it worked?* What if somehow they found Theodore and Gabe was the right man for her and the girls had such a warm community to grow up in and Danny cooperated? The people in Haven were behaving as if she could stay forever and be welcome. Would it be so wrong to see if they were right?

Hadn't life shown her enough to stop thinking in happy endings like that? Staying in Haven wasn't the best choice for her, and the flutter Gabe's eyes bloomed in her stomach didn't change that. *I can't trust my emotions here. The best thing would be to finish my ice cream without saying anything I can't take back.*

"I wish I had better news," Mike admitted to Gabe over coffee at Lila's Wednesday morning.

"You could have told me you'd hit dead ends over the phone." While Gabe was glad for time with his good friend, he'd assumed the request to meet meant either Mike had uncovered something about Theodore or his own team of attorneys had uncovered some loophole Harold had missed. He was wrong on both counts.

"I know this means a lot to you. I'm as frustrated as you are that your grandfather has disappeared into thin air."

I doubt that, Gabe thought bitterly. Mike was a longtime friend—one of his closest—but the failure to find Theodore wouldn't cost Mike anything but frustration. That same failure was starting to feel like it would cost Gabe everything. "I know," he conceded, not wanting the mounting tension to get to him. Gabe ran his hands down his face. "Is there anything else you can think of?"

Mike sighed. "I had my two best guys go through that will with a fine-tooth comb. I've run through the two best investigators I've got and every legal channel I can think of. Short of prayer, I don't know what else there is."

"We've got every soul in Haven praying for it now," Gabe admitted. He wouldn't admit—at least out loud—how he was getting pretty sore at the Almighty for leaving this hanging. The God he knew and loved would never let old Cyrus shaft a bunch of needy boys in order to build a silly strip mall. If he fought the urge to leave town if the whole thing went south, what must Avery be feeling? Right now he wouldn't be surprised if Avery was gone before sunup Monday morning—if not before the end of the doomed "celebration" party.

"What about the strip-mall thing?" Gabe asked in desperation. "Can we get an injunction or something to stave that off?"

"I thought of that. Even looked for a zoning loophole. I hate to say it, but Cyrus was pretty clever on this one. If there's a way to stop his 'incentive,' I haven't found it yet."

Gabe stared into his coffee, feeling as dark as the brew. This was going to hurt everyone involved, and they'd dragged Avery and her girls into the middle of it.

"But that doesn't mean I won't stop trying. We've still got four days. And the Gabe Everett I know doesn't give up." Mike sat back against the booth. "The Gabe Everett I know also would never invite a trio of females—two of them children, no less—into the sanctity of his home. How's that going?"

Well, there was a question. "I expect if you ask the six people in my house you'll get six different answers."

Mike never did fall for any of Gabe's diversions. "I'm asking *you*. Something's different about you."

"I'm stressed, I'm surrounded by pink, my house is in total chaos and I'm behind on four different schedules. Take your pick."

Mike narrowed his eyes. "Well, sure, I knew the kids would stress you out. Little ones have never been your thing. But that's not it. You're stressed, but the Gabe I know gets all hard and sharp when he's stressed. You're…" Mike grinned. "Well, to be honest, you got a bit of warm and fuzzy comin' up around the edges."

Gabe was suddenly thunderstruck by the ludicrous thought: Did it show? Could people actually see the way he felt like he was walking around with his chest cracked open? "It's nothing." He knew the minute he said it that Mike wasn't convinced. Maybe that was the real reason his friend had made the trip out here "on his way to Austin."

"Come on, Gabe. You know me better than to think I'll fall for that. What aren't you telling me?"

Gabe felt embarrassed that he actually checked the booths on either side of them to ensure they were empty. Haven had big ears and even bigger mouths some days. "It's…well, it's her." He followed the words with a pleading look, hoping Mike wouldn't laugh out loud.

"The mom? Avery Culpepper?"

Rather than confirm, Gabe offered Mike a helpless look. Gabe had, in fact, watched Mike gain the same helpless look over his current wife.

"I'm, um, she…" He couldn't even bring himself to admit it.

Mike leaned in. "Wait a minute—are you telling me you're falling for Avery Culpepper?" He leaned back with an examining eye as Gabe was powerless to deny it. The crack in his chest opened so wide it practically hurt. Every wailing country song about heartache made far too much sense to him these days.

"It's such a bad idea," he finally spit out. "We've dragged her and the girls into a calamity. She'll never stay, and I couldn't blame her a bit. I mean, come on—the timing, the circumstances, the little girls…"

Mike was stifling a chuckle under an entirely too-fake cough. "Well, what do you know? I wasn't sure it would ever happen, to tell you the truth."

"I'm miserable. You know me. I don't do kids and family. I definitely don't do little girls. This can't possibly work out—everybody will end up hurt."

The sharp tone knocked the amusement from

Mike's face. "Hey, I get it. You, me? We didn't get role models. Nobody in your family or mine would ever be up for Father of the Year. It's easy to think it's in the blood, I know. Only I never could quite understand why you looked at my happiness like some prize you could never win. We don't have to be the men our fathers were. With the right woman, we could be anything. I know I feel that way about Terri. Why not Avery?"

Gabe waited for the world to tilt. For some horrible thing to happen now that he'd admitted his attraction to Avery Culpepper to another living soul. Nothing. The world seemed to accept it far easier than he had.

"I can't make sense of it, Mike. I can't be anything close to what she needs. I can't make the pieces fit."

"You think this stuff ever goes by sense?" Mike fiddled with the gold band on his left hand. Gabe had been his best man when Mike acquired that ring. "I could give you twenty reasons why Terri and I shouldn't be together. I expect she could give you thirty. You're looking for order that won't ever come, buddy. But it's the best kind of miserable there is. Does Avery feel the same way?"

Gabe wished Mike hadn't asked that. The answer seemed to make it all so much more unsettling. "Maybe. There are moments, you know? The way she looks at me. She put her hand on my shoulder the other night and I thought I'd keel over right off the porch." He hadn't planned on sharing that, but it seemed to rush out of him through the ever-widening crack in his chest. No matter how he tried, this whole situation wouldn't stay within the neat lines he'd drawn around it, and that had to mean it was wrong.

"You do have it bad." Mike sighed. "Always figured that when you fell, you'd fall hard."

"She's leaving next week, Mike. And she should leave. She keeps saying she's got a job and a life back in Tennessee. Why ever would she stay in Haven after the whole Cyrus mess on the twentieth—and it will be one huge mess if we don't find Theo."

"You act like there's no convincing her to stay. You said it yourself—she seems to like it here. She'd need the girls' father's permission, yes, but I've seen it happen. It's not an impossible situation."

Gabe slumped back against the booth. "Even if I could convince her—and I'm not saying I could— would it really matter without Theo? She's told me she hates the idea of living under Cyrus's shadow. Could I really ask her to stay here with the awful stuff that will happen? Would you want to raise Mikey in that kind of family baggage? I can't deny her the chance to walk away from this craziness and go back to the life the girls know."

"What about a life the girls want? What Avery wants? What you finally figured out you want? So you'll let the memory of Cyrus Culpepper and the disappearance of your slippery old grandpappy cheat you out of your happiness? Now who's choosing to live under a shadow?" Mike checked his watch. "You're better than this, Gabe. You're stronger than this, and I, of all people, know that. I've got to head to my meeting in Austin, but that doesn't mean I'm slacking up on this with you. She could be the best thing to happen to you. But you'll never know if you let her slip through your fingers, crazy bequest or no crazy bequest." He stood up, gathering his coat. "As a matter of fact—"

"Mr. Boots!" Dinah's voice clamored from behind Gabe in the restaurant. Mike smiled broadly while Gabe gulped. He turned to see Dinah, Debbie and Avery walking toward him.

"We got your note," Dinah said.

Gabe stood and made the quickest introduction possible. Mike's grin was making him so squirrelly he nearly forgot to ask what she meant. "What note?"

"The one you left telling us to meet you here after Debbie's cast was on."

Debbie held up her neon pink, casted arm, wiggling her fingers out of one end. "Doc Delgado was right—it's all kinds of pretty colors now. But just a little broke."

"Brok*en*," Avery amended. "And you left a note on our car in front of Dr. Delgado's asking us to meet you here."

Mike's grin took on epic proportions. "Wasn't me," Gabe offered.

"Well, you're here now," Mike said cheerfully. He motioned toward the side of the booth he'd just vacated. "And I was just leaving before Gabe here had any chance at dessert. Have you had the pie here yet, girls?"

"Twice," Debbie announced as she slid into the seat without hesitation. Gabe watched his planned trip to the bank and supply store dissolve right before his eyes. He was already behind on five projects—would it really matter if he was behind in six?

Mike looked down at Debbie. "Excellent! I hear pie is very good for broken arms."

"Pie is very good for anything," Dinah declared as she slid in next to Gabe.

"You didn't ask us here?" Avery questioned, holding up a note. "You didn't put this on my windshield?"

Gabe peered at the note. Whoever had been "matchmaking" all over Haven had now set their sights on him and Avery. Just when he was thinking March couldn't get any worse.

Chapter Thirteen

Gabe had feared this moment since the day he had brought the box of swing parts onto the Five Rocks. He'd done everything he could think of to avoid it. He'd dodged several requests and had become an expert at creating urgent tasks whenever it looked as if the situation would arise.

And yet here he was, pushing Dinah on the swings Thursday morning.

Well, what did you expect when you put up a swing set? he lectured himself as Dinah settled herself gleefully onto the seat.

"Really high," Dinah requested.

"Medium high," Gabe responded, thinking Avery didn't need more reasons to visit Dr. Delgado. She and Debbie were there now, getting a checkup on Debbie's cast since her fingers were still looking puffy. As both girls were barred from the swing set until Debbie healed—a tactic even he could see as necessary since having one swing and one not would result in a torrent of tears—this was perhaps Dinah's last chance to play on the swings.

He'd agreed to the idea when it was Marlene and Jethro doing the pushing. Then Marlene's sister had one of her "emergencies"—that sister seemed to have dozens of crises, and always at the worst possible times—and the task had fallen to him.

At first he tried just watching. Supervising from the porch while Dinah pumped her tiny legs to no avail. He'd finally succumbed to the endless pleas of "Push me!" and found himself in his current predicament.

"Higher!" Dinah called.

"This is fine."

"Pleeeeaaaaasssseeee?" Surely, the world had no more irritating sound than a little girl's whine.

"Noooooooo," he responded as firmly as he dared without making his voice reflect the annoyance he felt.

This went on for twenty minutes. Any adult would be dizzy by now, Gabe thought, which gave him an idea. He slowed the swing to a stop, bringing a king-size moan from Dinah.

"Have you ever spun a swing?" He tried to make it sound exciting.

"Spun?"

He appealed to Dinah's sense of adventure. "You'll have to hold on real tight."

Her eyes lit up. "I can do that."

"You're sure now? I wouldn't want you to fall off."

She rolled her eyes. "I'm not Debbie."

Gabe was glad her mother wasn't here to hear that pint-size put-down. "Well, okay, if you're sure you can hold on."

Dinah replied by gripping the swing ropes with fierce determination.

Gabe spun Dinah around slowly, winding up the swing once or twice. "Ready?"

"Yup."

He let go, allowing the swing to spin at a slow speed, unwinding the twist he'd just made. The maneuver was decidedly tame, but it made her giggle just a bit.

"Phew!" he teased. "You made it."

"You're silly," she replied. "Do it again. Do it more."

That came as no surprise. "You're sure?"

"Spin it more!"

Gabe wound the swing six or seven times. "Hang on really tight now."

The swing unwound longer and slightly faster. Nothing even remotely dangerous, but he could see Dinah's eyes register a fair amount of dizziness when the swing finally stilled. She waited a moment—presumably for the world to stop swirling around her—before she looked up at him and said, "Again!"

"Okay, but this is the last time."

"Noooooo."

"Yes." He repeated the winding, mildly enjoying her squeals and giggles as the swing twisted itself free. She was definitely wobbly by the end.

"Again!"

"Stand up first." He got down on one knee in front of her, extending his arms for the inevitable. She stood up, and then promptly toppled over right into his arms. "And that's why we're stopping."

He'd expected her to refuse and squirm out of his arms, but instead she clung to him, laughing and settling into his embrace. The simple, open nature of her action bowled him over, and he found his arms going around her before he could stop them, hugging her tight.

When was the last time he'd hugged someone? Or someone hugged him? Sure, there had been social hugs or the standard cowboy clasps on the back, but to be hugged, clung to like this? There had been one woman in his life, years back, who always draped herself on him in a way that felt suffocating. That woman had accused him—rightly so—of being cold and distant. Nothing about Dinah's arms around his neck made him feel cold or distant. In fact, he wasn't rightly sure who was hugging who more tightly.

When had he become so walled off from people that touch had left his life? It made sense now why Avery's hand on his shoulder had bolted through him like a power surge.

"You're fun," Dinah said into the crook of his neck, snuggling closer. He told himself it was the dizziness that made her clutch him, but even he could see that for the lie that it was. She looked up at him. "Can you come home with us?"

The question smacked him in the chest. He sat back on the ground, bringing Dinah onto his lap.

"The swings can go home with you if you like. It's not like I'm going to use them."

"Yeah," she said, settling herself as if sitting on Gabe's lap was a perfectly natural thing to do. "Mom says we can bring them home. But can we bring you?"

Avery had said she would leave after the celebration, and he had no right to expect anything different from her.

Except that he did.

He'd somehow persuaded himself that they could stay, that they *should* stay. He didn't like the idea of Debbie and Dinah leaving Haven, leaving his life. He certainly didn't like the idea of Avery leaving his life. When he was honest, he didn't even take to the idea of their leaving Five Rocks. For all his annoyance at shoes in the hall, crayon on his papers and five juice spills a day, the house would seem empty without them.

Lonely.

Gabe was not a man who got lonesome. His houseguests were messing with his insides, and he wasn't sure what to do about it.

"Can you?" Dinah persisted.

Clearly, she had no idea of the size or implications of her question. He had to give her an answer, but was stumped for what to say. He opted for a standard evasive tactic—ask another question. "Do you miss home?"

"I miss my bed."

Gabe could commiserate. He'd never been much for traveling, preferring the comfort of his own familiar home. "I have a mighty fine bed. I'd miss it, too."

"I know. Debbie and I jumped on it when…" Her eyes went wide. "Oops. I wasn't supposed to tell."

The thought of those two jumping on the high, wide four-poster king-size bed in his room both amused and irritated him. Those girls had gotten just about everywhere in his house. "What else do you miss?" he asked, not wanting to venture a comment on his bed's use as a trampoline.

"I miss Dad."

Another big answer. It was the first time either of the girls had mentioned their father in front of him.

"He left." She said it with a heartbreaking sigh that made Gabe want to shake the clod of a man who had walked away from this family. The man who had Avery and gave her up was nothing short of a fool.

"I'm sorry for that," he said.

"Mama says he's still our dad."

"That's true," Gabe replied. "He'll always be your dad."

"We don't ever see him." The sad tone of her voice sunk a hole in Gabe's chest right in the spot where her little head lay resting.

"I'm sorry for that, too. I didn't see my daddy growing up, either." He found his arms tightening around the girl. "Shame something like that has to happen."

She looked up at him. "Do you think he'll come push me on the swings when we set 'em up back home?"

Those sweet little eyes could tear him to bits. Based on what Avery had told him, the answer was most likely no, which made that hole in his chest sink a mile deeper.

"I sure hope so" was all Gabe could manage to say. A fresh wave of resentment at the man fool enough to walk away from this family surged in his chest.

"Will you push me again?" Dinah asked.

Gabe said, "Absolutely," with no hesitation at all. He stood up and set Dinah on the ground in front of him. "But only until we hear Debbie and your mom coming up the drive. Then we'll have to stop."

"I know, 'cuz it's not fair." Dinah's bottom lip stuck out just the tiniest bit. "She can't swing."

"It won't be much longer," Gabe replied, consoling her as he began pushing. All the irritation had deflated right out of him thinking how Dinah had no dad who cared enough to push her on the swings. *It won't be much longer until they leave. This house will never feel the same,* Gabe thought as Dinah's giggles sailed across the spring breeze. He could never hope to be the kind of father Debbie and Dinah deserved, but today, now, he could be the kind of man who pushed a swing.

Avery and the girls were sorting flowerpots for celebration table decorations later that afternoon when Gabe walked by.

"How's the arm?" he asked Debbie.

She held up the bright pink cast. "Patching up."

"Good for you."

"The cast won't feel so tight once her swelling goes down some more. Doctor Delgado gave us the X-rays to take back to Tennessee. Six weeks in the cast," Avery added, "but she'll be fine by the time it's warm enough to swim." He resumed his walking until Avery stood up. "Gabe?"

"Yes?"

She'd thought hard about how to ask this, given the many implications. "I'd like to go look at the cabin again. Take a good look inside this time, and see what kind of shape it's in." It was a perfectly reasonable request, but given how many people seemed to think she ought to fix it up and move right in, she'd hesitated.

"You can do that anytime you like. Haverman gave you the keys, didn't he?"

"I...well, I'd like you to come with me." She started to add all the reasons why, but ended up silent.

He looked at her for a moment, rightly puzzled at her request.

She had to say something. "I know you're busy and everything, but... I just don't want to do it alone."

A warm understanding washed over his eyes. "I can take you up there." He paused for a moment, and she could see him deciding whether to say more. There was a whole delicate conversation hanging in the air, but with the way things were, and with the girls right there, it would have to remain unspoken.

"Tomorrow?" he asked, his voice unusually soft.

"That'd be just fine."

"I'll be in town most of the morning, but I can circle back and pick you up."

"No need. I've got some things to pick up in town myself, so I'll just meet you in town and we can drive out from there."

She wanted him there, but she didn't want him to take her there. She needed to do that part herself. Which made no sense. The line between standing on her own two feet and depending on Gabe was starting to blur, and that bothered her.

Because she was leaving when the weekend was over. At least she was mostly sure she was. It was getting harder to know what it was she wanted.

Chapter Fourteen

Avery walked out of the town hardware store Friday morning with a big bag of cleaning supplies. She could have borrowed all this from Gabe, but it felt better to purchase them on her own. The run-down cabin at the back of the Culpepper ranch property was hers now, so she should start to clean it up. Even if all she could do before she left was make a small dent, it would feel good to do *something*. It might help settle her mind about what to do next.

It would certainly be only a small dent, if that. The place looked to need a lot more than a good scrubbing to be either livable or sellable.

Pulling some juice boxes from her handbag, she lined the girls up on a park bench while she looked through the list of handymen that Tanner Barstow, the owner of the farm supply store, had given her.

Where to start? Avery pulled photos she'd taken of the property up on her cell phone. The pictures made her heart sink. She knew enough about houses to see that the place had good bones, but the fallen shingles, a boarded-up window and debris scattered about the foundation told her how much work was ahead of her. Or ahead of anyone she hired. *Well, maybe it will give me a reason to come back and visit*, she thought.

"That's ugly," Dinah said, swinging her feet as she sat on the bench sipping apple juice. "Who'd want to live there?"

"Nobody's lived there in a long time," Avery explained in optimistic tones. "It needs fixing up." She nervously fingered the keys to the place. "Mr. Boots is meeting us here. Then we'll drive over to the cabin to go inside and get started." She'd know for sure once she was inside, but it was a good guess the place needed major structural repairs. Could she sell it in its current shape? Would anyone even buy it? They'd be more likely to tear it down, and that felt wrong. Her grandfather had grown up there—it was the closest thing to roots she could claim.

If someone hadn't claimed it first—and by "someone," she meant a snake, or a possum, or any number of varmints she'd imagined might have taken up residence in the abandoned home.

She peered at the photo again, as if it would hold clues to anything living inside. At best, she'd encounter trash and disrepair. At worst…well, let's just say that was another reason not to have to enter alone. Maybe she should have left the girls at home for this trip.

Avery looked up to see a familiar old man crossing the street. Wasn't that Harley Jones?

"Hello, Mr. Jones!" she called, wanting to be friendly. After all, Gabe had said Mr. Jones lived in an old cabin at the back of Gabe's property. Maybe he knew a thing or two about bringing an old cabin up to snuff.

He turned, startled. As if surprised anyone would say hello to him.

"How are you today?" she asked.

"Same as any other day."

Maybe he didn't recall who she was. "I'm Avery Culpepper. We're guests of Gabe's at Five Rocks."

"I remember," he said, his sour face softening a bit. "And these are…" His face scrunched up into a collection of weathered wrinkles as she could see him trying to remember the girls' names. "Starts with *D*'s…"

"I'm Debbie."

"And I'm Dinah."

He almost grinned. Not quite, but almost. "You're sure now? You could be switching 'em on me and I'd never know."

Avery laughed. "No, they gave you the right names." She slanted a glance toward Dinah. "Not that they haven't tried that particular trick on some other folks." She sighed and held up the photo on her phone. "We're meeting Gabe here to go check out the inside of my new property."

Harley squinted at the phone display and scratched his chin. "Ain't much to look at, is she?"

"Are you a cowboy?" Debbie asked. She'd begun to ask that of anyone wearing a cowboy hat. While some of the answers she received were amusing, Avery was wondering if the charm was wearing off. Harley certainly didn't look amused, but then again she'd never seen him looking like anything but as if he'd just bitten a lemon.

"We're from Tennessee," she offered by way of explanation, which really wasn't much of a reason for a state that boasted the country music capital of the world.

Harley leaned on his cane to stare at Debbie. "Ain't they got cowboys up there in Tennessee?"

"They got cowboy *hats*," Debbie said, completely unfazed by the old man's gruff demeanor. "But anyone could wear those."

Harley chuckled. "Oh, well, you're right there. The hat does not necessarily make the man." He turned to Avery. "Sharp girls you got there, ma'am. You're Cyrus's granddaughter. The real one, I hear tell."

Avery shrugged. "That's me." Why did everyone feel compelled to remind her someone had tried to step into her identity—and her inheritance? Considering the state of the cabin, it made the whole scheme seem that much more absurd. Who'd go to such lengths to get their hands on that mess? No one knew if there was anything more to her inheritance, least of all her.

"Whole thing's a mess, that's what it is. Only now with you here, it'll mostly shake itself out, I suppose."

Avery remembered the silhouette of Gabe hunched in defeat against the porch column. "Well, not necessarily."

"But you're here."

"Yes, but I'm only one of the stipulations." It still sounded crazy, no matter now many times she said it. "There are still the four original residents of the boys ranch to find. They've found three—and me, of course—but unless they find the last one, it won't matter. Without Gabe's grandfather, it won't matter how many of the other requirements they've met. Cyrus made sure it was an all-or-nothing proposition."

That seemed to agitate the old man. Which was understandable—even Avery couldn't understand why her grandfather had gone to such extremes. She was glad he eased himself down on the bench beside her. "Find Theodore Linley? He's long gone. They won't hold anyone to such nonsense."

"From what I hear, they have to. Seems my dear old grandfather locked the whole thing down tight— legally speaking, that is. If they don't find this man and bring him to the party, then the Triple C becomes a strip mall and the boys ranch has to go back to the Silver Star."

"They'd never do that." He shook his head. "Strip mall? And send half the boys elsewhere? That's fool talk. It won't never come to that."

"They'll have no choice." She sat back against the bench. "A strip mall, can you imagine? My grandpa Cyrus was one wily old coot."

Harley worried at his cane handle with one gnarled hand. "You're tellin' me all that happens if that Linley fellow don't show?"

"Sad, isn't it?" Avery pulled a box of animal crackers from her bag and handed it to the girls. "It's tying Gabe into knots that he can't find any trace of the man."

"Nonsense. That isn't Gabe's fault."

"You and I can see that. And it seems pretty clear to me the guy doesn't want to be found or is long dead—but Gabe sure blames himself."

Harley turned his face to look down the street.

"Takes a lot on himself, Gabe does." His tone was so sad.

"He speaks very fondly of you," she offered. The poor man probably considered himself a burden the way Danny's grandmother had in her last days. She hadn't been. She was a sweet woman who almost made Avery feel like she had a family. She hated how Danny's actions were teaching Debbie and Dinah that family was something that could be discarded when it became inconvenient. That's not how family should ever work. Not that she'd experienced much to the contrary.

Harley kept staring down the street. "Does he now?"

She remembered how often Gabe went to visit Harley with food or just to keep him company, and tenderly touched the old man's elbow. "I think you're actually quite dear to him, but you know Gabe—I doubt he'd ever come out and tell you."

That sent Harley into a chuckle that all too quickly dissolved into a rasping cough. Dinah sweetly held up her apple juice to share with the man, but he waved her off and began to struggle to his feet. "I'm sure Gabe'll be here any minute. I'd best get on."

"You're sure? You can sit with us a spell. We can give you a ride back to Five Rocks."

His face took on the sour, tight countenance she'd seen almost all the time from him. "I got my own car. I ain't so far gone that I can't get myself to town and back, young lady."

The girls looked up at his sharp tone, and he seemed to realize how harsh his words had been. "You all come tell me what you found in there one of these days," he said, backpedaling and trying to show a sliver of a smile. "I expect it'll be quite a story."

"Oh, I hope not," Avery replied. Dinah and Debbie made dual slurping sounds as they finished up their juice boxes just as Gabe's truck pulled around the corner.

"Tell Gabe I said hello," Harley called as he started down the block.

"You sure you don't want to stay and say hello yourself?" He couldn't have so much to do that an extra five minutes would be so much of a burden. Harley had to be lonely, living all the way on the back of Five Rocks all by himself.

"Nope," he called abruptly over his shoulder, picking up the pace of his labored hobbling.

What was that all about? Was Harley avoiding Gabe? Had the remark about Gabe's fondness for the old man crossed some sort of line with him?

For a small simple town, Avery thought to herself, *Haven sure is complicated.*

Avery was trying to put up a good front as she stood inside the mess of a house. She was trying to act as if inheriting this pile of lumber was a good thing. Based on what Gabe saw today, he might just tear the whole thing down if he was in her place.

She stood in the empty front room, staring at the dented, crumbling walls. "It has good bones," she declared.

Bones? he thought. No one could want to live in this skeleton. Cyrus hadn't done her any favors by leaving her this. It'd take a year's worth of work—and a wheelbarrow full of money—to make this place anything anyone would ever want. Another reason she had every right to head on back to Tennessee come Monday.

"You going to sell the place?" he asked.

"Of course," she replied quickly. "It makes no sense to keep it. We have a home in Tennessee."

Yes, she did. The fact seemed to follow him around like a shadow. He'd already come to dread the moment she would leave Five Rocks and return to Tennessee. The selfish part of him wanted her nearby, wanted her to be a part of Haven.

But in two days, she'd have no reason to stay. Everything felt like it was slipping through his fingers.

"Look, Mama!" Debbie had opened a closet door and pulled out a musty old afghan.

The large blue square was falling apart, but Gabe could still make out the faded design stitched into the center. "That's Cyrus's brand," he said, outlining the design with his finger. "I wonder if June made it."

Avery held out her hands for the relic. "June Culpepper? My grandmother?"

"She was always knitting things, I recall. Every church bazaar had a dozen hats or throws from her. Before she passed, that is."

"It smells funny," Dinah said, wrinkling her nose.

"It's very old," Avery said, touching it with a sad tenderness. "And not in good shape. I expect it's been in the bottom of that closet for decades." She pulled at one piece of the fringe and a whole corner of the afghan seemed to unravel in her hands. Avery whimpered as if wounded.

She had next to nothing from her family, and here she had to watch something crumble before her eyes.

It seemed cruel. "Maybe we can save the design," he offered, having no idea if such a thing was possible. Avery had a trunkful of cleaning supplies, but they'd given up any hope of starting that within five minutes of opening the door. This house didn't need a dustpan, it needed a shovel. Maybe even a backhoe.

Gabe removed the cleaning supplies from the box Avery had brought and held it out. "Put it in here," he said as gently as he could. "You can take it to Marnie over at the ranch and see what she can do. She does all kinds of yarn stuff and if anyone knows how to save it, she will." He understood the sentiment. He had a ratty old football jersey of his father's, and that chair of his mother's—and he'd be beside himself if anything happened to either of those. Even family you resented was still family, and everybody deserved at least a piece of their roots.

The tattered afghan seemed to unhinge something in Avery. She'd kept up a nervously optimistic attitude the whole time they'd been in the house, but he could practically watch her lose the ability to keep that up. Her shoulders fell forward, she began to pace the empty room and her lips pressed together.

He felt for her, he truly did. Cyrus had put her through the ringer with all this business, and he admired that she'd held up as well as she had. It felt unfair that the one solid thing she'd gotten out of this whole mess so far was a tumble-down house that right now was more of a burden than a blessing.

"Why'd he do any of this?" She was trying not to lose it in front of the girls—even he could see that. Should he stay beside her, or invent some reason to take the girls outside and let her go to pieces alone?

Alone seemed the worse of the two, so Gabe reached out and put a hand on her shoulder. The act unleashed a short sob from her, one of Avery's delicate hands flying up to cover her mouth as if she could hold it all in.

He couldn't answer Avery's frustrated question—no one could.

It was the wrong thing to do. It would confuse the girls and cross a dozen boundaries, but Gabe could no more stand there and watch Avery unravel than he could have left her there on Roz's porch. He pulled Avery toward him, feeling her composure fall away as she dissolved against his chest and cried. Not pretty, careful tears, but great, reckless sobs that made her shoulders shake and her fists grab at his sleeves.

"Don't cry, Mama. It's not that ugly in here." Dinah's heartbreakingly tender voice came from down beside them.

Avery, of course, cried all the harder at her daughter's attempt at comfort. At another time, he might have found her misguided grasp of the situation amusing, but there was no humor in today. He wrapped his arms more tightly around Avery, startled by the sense of honor and purpose that enveloped him as he did so. Gabe felt Dinah and Debbie circle around his and Avery's legs in a tiny huddle that made his own heart twist in a surge of care and sympathy.

He'd stand here and let her cry it out because no one should have to do this alone. And because he wanted to be the one to hold her up while she fell to pieces. He wanted to lend her his strength, to shield her in this overwhelming moment.

Gabe let one hand fall softly on her hair, soothing

as she cried against him. He couldn't explain why the awful moment felt right, sacred even. These three people had come to mean so much more to him than the solution to the problem Cyrus had dumped on him and all of Haven. But he also knew, with a certainty he'd been denying for weeks now, that he didn't want them to go. Not after Sunday, not ever.

Avery pulled her hands from his sleeves to wrap them tightly around his chest, clinging to him with a desperation that broke his heart wide open. For a moment, he allowed himself the indulgence of laying his chin against the top of her head, reveling in the way she tucked perfectly inside his embrace.

It was the exquisite opposite of being alone.

He wanted to kiss that soft brown hair. He wanted to kiss away the tears and make promises he couldn't keep. Irrational promises that she wouldn't have to do any of this alone or ever be alone again.

Such promises would only make things worse for her. And so Gabe said nothing—not because he didn't want to speak his fumbling words of comfort to her, but because Avery deserved to hear eloquent words from a man who would woo her and cherish her the way a lifetime bachelor like himself could never hope to do. He'd choke on his own silence before he added to the line of men who'd disappointed her.

But oh, how unwise promises and declarations roared in his chest, clawing against her heartbeat to set traps for the both of them. While strong and stubborn, she'd pulled a surprising admiration from him. While weak and broken, however, Avery had gone and stolen his heart.

And it was gone, he realized. He'd lost the battle

to deny what he felt for her. For all three of them. He loved her.

As he held her, the thought fixed itself clear and true in his head. He loved her. But that thought came with the equally clear truth that he would love her alone. He would love her enough to give her the happiness she'd never have with him. Life had made him a creature of privacy and distance, not the rest-of-your-life family man she needed and deserved. He would bear her tears today, and be honored to do so, but he would also bear her leaving. He would never, ever risk being the source of her sadness.

It seemed to Gabe that he'd lived an hour in the span of minutes he'd held her, that time had stopped until she pulled away, embarrassed and sniffling. Even Debbie and Dinah looked up at him with tearful, confused eyes.

"It's okay," Avery said, squatting down to gather the girls in her arms.

Gabe looked down and fought the urge to pull all three of them right back into his arms. The massive hole in his chest was permanent as of this moment—they'd taken a piece of him he'd never get back.

Chapter Fifteen

All Saturday morning, Avery and Gabe had maneuvered around each other with a careful distance. No one wanted to admit the lines that had been crossed back there in the dirty cabin. No one wanted to talk about the goodbye that had to happen soon. No one had found Linley. Avery felt as if the whole house crackled with tension on multiple levels.

She fled for a bit to the boys ranch, to drop off the afghan with Marnie and pick up some mason jar lanterns that were being redecorated and repurposed from the ranch's Thanksgiving banquet. The ranch was buzzing with cautiously optimistic preparations, but somehow she didn't feel much like joining in, knowing she'd be leaving all this behind in a matter of days.

She'd just pulled the last box from her trunk when she heard it—a loud, hard series of whacks. Bangs so loud it was a wonder the whole house didn't shake. Jethro had taken the twins "fishing"—which basically meant he took the girls and a basket of cookies out to the tiny creek where no one ever caught any fish, but no one ever seemed to mind—and Marlene was sorting linens.

Whack. Tumble. Whack. Grunt. It was something out by the barn where Gabe was, and it was far from peaceful. It was angry. Fierce. If the tension of the house had a sound, this was it.

That meant it was something she should probably avoid, but when she heard a sharp cry of pain, Avery put down her box and walked cautiously toward the barn.

She found Gabe stalking around a pile of logs, an axe sunk into one large stump. He had his back to her and was grumbling in dark and sour tones. When he turned a bit, Avery noticed he cradled his left hand in a bandana.

"Gabe?"

He looked up at her with a wild storm in his eyes. Why were they always finding each other in the midst of their wit's end? She and Gabe seemed to collide at the worst possible moments, repeated witnesses to each other's pain.

"I'm fine," he barked.

She almost had to laugh at that. "You are not."

"I just got a sliver, that's all."

Gabe Everett was a huge man. No piddly sliver would make him hold his hand like that. Were it not for the lack of blood, she'd assume his axe went through a finger from the way he grimaced.

"Should I call Marlene?"

He glowered at the idea. "Absolutely not."

She looked around at the huge pile of chopped wood. It was springtime, but he'd chopped enough for two winters. This clearly wasn't about fuel, so it wasn't hard to guess what was going on. "Taking out your frustrations on innocent tree parts?"

She'd hoped the small joke would take some of the dark edge off his features, but it didn't. At least he stopped his furious pacing. "Some."

Avery ventured a step closer. "Did it work?"

"Does it look like it worked?"

"Not a bit, actually." The last week had wound Gabe so tight she was surprised he hadn't done something more drastic than chop wood. The anniversary deadline arrived tomorrow, and watching Gabe Everett stare failure in the face was a gut-wrenching sight. "Look, Gabe, surely you know no one blames you for—"

"Don't!" he snapped before she could finish the sentence, the word so sharp and loud it made her jump. He'd grown so kind and gentle with her and the girls she'd forgotten just how imposing a man he was.

He saw her jump and cringed, then simply sank down onto a nearby log. "Just don't, okay?"

What comfort could she hope to offer? Over the last week she'd watched Gabe try every possible source, spend untold sums of money, call in favors and generally do every conceivable thing to find Theodore Linley.

And fail.

The man had virtually vanished off the face of the earth, and all those young boys would pay the price. *Unfair* didn't begin to do the situation justice.

She pointed to the hand. "Does it hurt?"

"It's nothing."

"Oh, I doubt that." He was holding it like it would

drop off at any second. "You didn't cut off a finger or anything, did you?"

"I told you, it's just a sliver." He'd been pushing everyone away for hours, evidently determined to face this failure alone.

No one should have to do this alone. "Then you won't mind showing me."

"As a matter of fact, I would mind."

"Tough."

That raised an eyebrow. She'd never challenged him before—she got the impression few people ever did. When he didn't warn her off, she walked closer, sat down next to him and held out her hand with her best "do what you're told" mother glare.

Gabe surprised her by complying. She unfolded the bandana to find a startlingly large shard of wood embedded in the base of his thumb.

"If that's a 'sliver,' the girls have gone whaling. Gabe, there's half a tree in there!"

"I've had worse."

"Well, don't you think you should get it out?"

"I was *about to* before I was interrupted. Want to watch? You know, in case I keel over or anything?" It was dark, sour teasing, but at least the near-lethal edge was fading from his eyes.

She cringed. "Not particularly." This looked like no mere "put a bandage on it and kiss it better" injury. The man looked as if he might need stitches.

"Tough," he said, throwing her own word back at her with a victorious gleam. Then, without preparation or ceremony, he simply grabbed the chunk of wood with his teeth and yanked it out of his thumb with a blood-chilling hiss. Avery felt her head swim a bit at so brutal a remedy.

It was clear the removal hurt tremendously, but he wasn't going to show it. His jaw worked and he flexed and shook the wounded hand as he spit the offending wood away with a growl. She'd probably either be crying or have fainted from such a yank, but Gabe just looked steamed. Tense and angry. Even in pain—emotional or physical—the man refused to lower his guard. *It must be exhausting to live like that*, she thought.

And yet, he'd been so kind to her when her own guard had fallen. It had come crashing down back at the cabin, surely. Gabe had been wonderful in those moments. Strong and protective and loyal—exactly what she needed, what she'd been missing for so long. The memory made heat rise up her spine. He was there for everyone else but let no one be there for him. That was as unfair as all this business with the will.

"Better?" she said softly, nodding her head into his view even as he gripped his now-bleeding thumb with his other hand.

"No," he growled, turning away from her.

It was the closest thing to an admission of pain she'd ever got from him. It wasn't better—neither the wound nor the search for Linley. There wasn't really any better to be had.

Avery knew, just by looking at him, that both would leave a scar.

She picked up the bandana off his knee and reached for his hand. He resisted. She tugged at him anyway, pulling the injured hand toward her lap and wrapping the bandana tight over the wound. "Put pressure on it. And you should go inside and wash that up before it gets infected."

He didn't move. Instead, he stayed stock-still and stared at her. Fighting, she could see, to keep the wall up between them while everything else tumbled down around him. Hadn't she been doing the same thing? She felt her heart scrambling in her chest, desperate to come open, fighting against her determination to keep it locked up tight.

"It hurts," he admitted, and she knew those two words cost him everything to speak. They were both so achingly weary, wounded in so many ways by this fiasco Cyrus had launched. It felt like a trap neither of them deserved.

She stared at the wounded thumb, then back up at the storm in his eyes. She did what any mother would do. She brought up Gabe's hand, cradled it in both of her hands and kissed it. Avery knew exactly what she was doing and why it shouldn't happen, but there was no stopping it. She wanted, even if only for this moment, to lay the battle down. To make even this tiny part of it better, if only just for now.

It crossed the line they'd carefully drawn between them, and they both knew it. She had opened her heart—partially back at the cabin, but fully at this moment. It made it hard to breathe; both exhilaration and anxiety swirled around her at the same time.

Avery looked up from the wounded hand to stare into Gabe's eyes. She made herself hold his gaze, to meet him in this moment, no matter how hard her heart pounded. She could see the precise moment his armor fell away, the change so dramatic in his eyes that it was as if they changed color. Storm clouds to blue sky. The man she'd barely glimpsed out by the toolboxes showed up now in full force; an overpowering, stunning transformation that stilled her pulse. A man far more tender than everyone else saw, but somehow far more powerful for that tenderness. A man who loved as fiercely as he fought.

Gabe felt like he was falling off some high cliff or diving into some fast-running river. Everything he'd tried so hard to keep from happening—the surge in his heart, the nonstop need to know where Avery was and if she was okay, the confounding affection for those little girls—happened anyway. He should stop it, but he couldn't. Worse yet, right now he didn't want to. Wouldn't it be wonderful to let himself really hold her? Kiss her the way he was aching to. Tell her she should never have to be alone again and lie to himself that he could be the man to make that happen.

Gabe was many things, but he never counted being weak among them. The power of his will was his greatest asset. He bent circumstances and people to his need or the greater good all the time. Served his community tirelessly, fought for causes, supervised a large and successful ranch.

And yet he'd never felt as weak, as downright powerless, as he did right now. There simply wasn't any hope for it. He couldn't make his mind or even his arms resist despite nearly yelling at himself silently in his head.

Gabe pulled Avery close to him, and when she lifted her sweet face toward his, he kissed her. The absolute delight of it nearly consumed him. After so many days of trying not to wonder how those lips tasted, the glory of tasting her nearly knocked him over. *Glory*. That was the only word he could think of—when he managed to think at all—for what it felt like.

Avery made a tiny sound and slipped her hands around his neck, and Gabe was lost. He knew it would take a hundred years to gather up the will to stop. The girls or Marlene or anyone could come around the corner of the barn at any second and Gabe couldn't bring himself to care. It felt as though kissing her was like pure oxygen and he'd spent the last weeks gasping for breath.

She was leaving, and everything around him was about to fail. The rightness of holding her—of the way his heart seemed to reach toward her, of how he felt her beside him even when they were clear across the room—was the only balm to make that pain subside. He desperately needed it, even if only for a few moments. Kissing her, having her look into his eyes the way she just had, made him feel as if he could do anything. He was unstoppable. Victorious despite the defeat that was poised to come down on his head.

He needed her, more than he felt capable of denying himself. Her sweet heart called to him stronger than his own will, and that scared him to death. He ought to push her away, end this exquisite kiss and tell her to go back to her life in Tennessee, but he couldn't. He wasn't capable of it. He didn't even want to be capable of pulling away from her.

She proved him right, pulling away first with a gasping breath he felt through every corner of his chest. "Gabe," she said, his name more of a breath than a word. Nothing could have undone him more than to hear her say his name that way with that look in her eyes.

I'm not who she needs, he pleaded with his reason. *It can't matter that I need her.* It couldn't matter that he felt like he'd been wandering through his days at everyone else's service and just now woke up to what he really wanted.

Because what he wanted—more than anything, more than was wise, far more than was good for any of them—was her. In his life, gazing at him like that every day.

He feathered his good hand against the porcelain rose of her cheeks, flushed by the rush of what had just passed between them. Sure, right now it felt as if he'd sooner die than walk away from her, but that was too marvelous to stick. The glowing in his chest couldn't be trusted, even if it was love. Parenting was hard work even when you were born to it. He'd never had those instincts, never wanted to have them. His quiet and order were how he survived—how would he live with tiny pinkness messing things up year after year? A whole life of solitude couldn't just transform in the space of a month. Sooner or later he'd have to own up to what he knew to be his true nature.

Tomorrow, he'd pay the piper for every failing.

Tonight, he'd kiss her. Again. And memorize every detail of it to make it last after he sent her away.

He'd fail at that, too. He knew, even as he settled his mouth against her impossibly soft lips, that it'd never be enough. He would wish for more of her every day of his life from here on in.

Chapter Sixteen

The anniversary celebration was by far the oddest affair Avery had ever attended. The whole thing felt like a warped blend of birthday party and funeral luncheon. Everyone wandered around the beautifully decorated barn with an air of tense happiness. There was laughter, groaning-full tables of good food, cheery hellos and handshakes, but it all glossed over the huge disappointment everyone knew was coming.

After that heart-stopping set of kisses yesterday, Gabe had pulled himself away and walked without a word into the house. She'd sat on the log for a few moments, desperately trying to sort out her feelings. Should she leave? Could she even consider staying? What she felt now, strong as it was, didn't change a single one of the obstacles facing her. It certainly couldn't be enough to risk the girls' stability.

But what about their happiness? Hers? She had wandered inside, lost in a haze of emotion and confusion. Gabe's study door was shut and she couldn't bring herself to open it. What was there to say or do?

He didn't come out for supper. She could barely keep up the appearance of an appetite herself.

Sunday morning, Gabe left before everyone else rose and stayed away until timing forced his return to dress for the late-afternoon party.

She left him alone. It wasn't as if she could help what was about to happen. Last night had been a wonderful mistake, but a mistake anyway. She needed to leave. Even if she could somehow stay, if Danny consented to let her move the girls, would she really want to? Build a life as living embodiment of what Cyrus had done to this community? Back in Tennessee, she wouldn't have to watch them tear that beautiful old estate down to put in a strip mall. Watch them send boys back to places that weren't as beautiful or special as the Triple C. It hurt to leave, but not as much as standing in this party and pretending to be happy—her heart was breaking on so many levels.

Bea pulled Avery from her thoughts by clanging a spoon against a glass. The woman stood in the center of a little makeshift stage at one end of the barn, framed in dried vine arrangements Avery had helped to make.

"I'm delighted to say that the boys have prepared a little entertainment for y'all this afternoon."

Dinah tugged on her hand. "Do we get to see a show?"

"I don't know what we'll get to see," Avery replied. "You'll just have to wait and find out like the rest of us." She pointed to the stage, where the boys lined up in a bumbling sort of line, each holding a sheet of paper.

The tallest boy—Riley, she remembered from

her time painting frames with the boys—stepped to the microphone. "We have a poem for you. Nothing fancy, but y'all might find it interesting. On account of most of you are in it."

"That can't be good," Jethro muttered beside Avery.

"Hush now, they might surprise you," Marlene chided.

Riley cleared his throat and smoothed his page on the podium, then began.

> "Some folks think we're not much good,
> "That ranch boys ain't got smarts.
> "But we see more than you might think
> "When it comes to lonely hearts."

"Well, this just got interesting," Marlene whispered.

Riley stepped away as Avery recognized Ben moving up to the podium.

> "Mr. Tanner may sell seed,
> "Or tractors, hay or twine,
> "But it took more than books before
> "He read between the lines!"

One of the youngest held up one of the painted frames—filled not with a boy's photograph, but with a red paper heart that read "Tanner + Macy" in big letters. He hung the frame by a colored ribbon to the decorative vines. The room burst into laughter and applause at the poem and the antics it confessed. The boys were the mystery matchmakers, it seemed.

"I suspected it was you," Macy announced.

"You did not," Ben countered, smiling all the while.

"I thought my students wrote me *not* to take up with Tanner!" Macy called as Tanner's face turned more than a few shades red.

"Well, they did, but they got a little help from us, too. Changed our mind about that, didn't we?" Ben called back.

"They do say teamwork is the first tool of management," Harold Haverman called playfully to Tanner. "Gotta respect a young man who changes his thinking and makes use of resources."

"Not in my Sunday school class I don't," Macy called back. "Y'all stop such meddling."

"No need to meddle anymore now," Ben replied. "I'd say we got the job done."

"Oh, so *you're* taking credit for this?" Tanner teased.

"Only some. Most, maybe."

That sent the room into further laughter as Ben left the podium and Diego and Stephen took their place. In tandem, they recited:

"Miss Josie may be fond of calves,
"But Rangers take her heart.
"So we sent pie and baby things
"To give those two a start."

Another frame, this one holding a "Heath + Josie" heart, rose from the smallest of boys.

"That was a pretty good pie," Heath called out. "Surely, none of *you* made it."

"Another bit of teamwork," Lila from the café added with a wide smile. "Who could resist helping out a cause like that?"

"You could have at least spelled my name right on your note." Heath pointed a finger at the boys.

"Nobody's perfect, amigo." Diego offered an exaggerated wink as he stepped away from the podium.

Avery gaped at Marlene as a trio of the younger boys took to the podium for another recitation.

"Miss Lana had to kiss some frogs
"Before she got her prince
"But little Logan's Christmas wish
"Sure looked a lot like Flint's!"

"That's a terrible rhyme," Flint moaned, his hand over his eyes as the now-expected framed heart appeared and was hung on the vines.

"Honestly, you did some terrible matchmaking, boys," Lana added. She'd told Avery about the multiple notes pointing her in the direction of some truly unsuitable "matches."

"Hey, someone had to make sure Mr. Flint looked good by comparison," one of the boys said.

"Thanks for the vote of confidence," Flint commented with a mock sour look.

"It worked, didn't it?" a second boy called back.

"So all the mystery matchmaking you told me about—it was the ranch boys the whole time?" Avery asked Marlene.

"And they're three for three, those rascals," Marlene said, giggling.

Avery thought about the note she'd received invit-

ing her to pie at Lila's and gulped. The boys had caught
on to the attraction between her and Gabe, but they
wouldn't keep their "perfect score" today. How could
she explain to those boys—and everyone listening—
that in her and Gabe's case it wasn't enough?

It *wasn't* enough, was it?

Corey and Aiden, two other of the ranch boys,
stepped up to the podium, but Avery barely listened
to their poem about false invitations to a dance as
part of a rodeo fund-raiser. Her pulse was starting
to roar over what would happen when those boys got
to her and Gabe. They'd make some clever rhyme
about how they belonged together, and she couldn't
bear to hear it.

Because such a huge part of her had come to believe that she and Gabe did belong together. She
wanted to see a frame holding their names coupled.
She wanted to belong here, with these people, far
more than she wanted to go back to Tennessee.

But I can't, can I?

As laughter and applause rang out for Nick and
Darcy, Avery headed for the door. She couldn't hear
the next verse about the veterinarian, Wyatt, and his
long-lost love, Carolina. Nor could she bear to see
them leave off the last verse—or worse yet, speak
up—about their unsuccessful attempts at matching
her up with Gabe.

She fled out the back entrance to lean against the
side of the barn and gulp down air. *I can't stay. I can't
bear to leave. Lord, why ever did You bring me here?*

It would be complicated and messy to stay here.
She'd have to deal with Cyrus's legacy. She'd have
to watch the whole town shoulder this unfair bur-

den. She'd have to restart her business. She'd have to ask Danny for permission, and she chafed at the idea of asking him for anything, sure he'd say no just to spite her. None of those things seemed to matter in light of her heart.

For her heart had already chosen to stay here, whether she physically left or not. Her heart had fixed itself to the man about to tear out his own heart up on that stage surrounded by symbols of everyone else's happiness.

She couldn't leave him to do that alone. Not after all he'd done, after all he meant to the girls. To her. She'd go inside and stand witness to his pain. She owed him that much.

Chapter Seventeen

If a silence could roar in a man's ears, it was roaring in Gabe's. There was no doubt now who had slid the note under Avery's windshield. He and Avery had been the final target of the boys ranch matchmakers.

The final, failing target. He'd pulled the frame from the little boy's hand, silencing the final stanza of their little matchmaking skit, unable to bear whatever they planned to say.

What did it say if even teenagers picked up on the attraction between himself and Avery? Was the whole town watching them fight the pull between them? The idea made Gabe feel beyond vulnerable, made him want to disappear as totally as Theodore had done. The final empty spot on the stage vines—the spot where a frame bearing "Gabe + Avery" should have been—loomed like a black hole.

And here he thought today was already as awful a day as a man could stand.

It didn't help that he'd barely slept. The pair of kisses he'd shared with Avery burned so bright in his memory that sleep had been impossible. She'd ended their second kiss as she had their first, with a sigh of his name that cut through him. Only that second sigh was one of regret, or lost possibility, or just plain "it can never be." If God's timing was supposed to be perfect, it wasn't feeling one bit perfect at the moment. Everything felt the exact opposite of perfect.

Gabe had seen Avery leave the barn. Every bone in his body wanted to follow her, to escape this awful, gaping moment, but he couldn't. He still had one final wound to endure.

Every eye in the room was still staring at him as he set the offending frame facedown on the podium. His stomach turned somersaults over the bad news that was his job to declare. It wouldn't come as a surprise—everyone in town already knew Theodore Linley hadn't been found. That was bad enough. But to have to say it out loud? To tell the boys they'd have to pack up and move back to the old location? There wasn't a more loathsome task in the world right now.

Avery's words to him that first night on the ranch rang in his ears: *I hate him. I know I'm not supposed to, but I do.* Right now, at this moment, he hated Culpepper for toying with those boys' futures. For thinking any good whatsoever could come from the Triple C becoming a strip mall when it could be—had already become—the ranch's new home.

He hated Culpepper for forcing him to hunt for his grandfather, only to come up empty at everyone's expense.

How could Culpepper hang lives in a stupid balance like he had? His own pain was bad enough, but boys would now have to be turned away, for crying out loud.

I hate you. Gabe had always tried to steer clear of words like *hate*, but such moderation evaded him now. Hate, regret and disappointment boiled in his gut.

Gabe cleared his throat, words escaping him. He'd rehearsed this dreaded speech over and over last night, but nothing suited this tragedy. Because that's what it was—a regrettable, preventable tragedy brought about by old men who cared nothing for the generation after them.

"Well," he began, not able to look any of the boys or house parents in the eye, "y'all know the task... handed to us." His heart wanted to yell and stomp and call it an underhanded scheme, but the only gift he could give this crowd right now was to avoid stooping to Cyrus's level. "And I'm proud of how our little community pulled together to rise to the challenge. Bea found Samuel Teller, and we're glad to have you here, Sam. Heath found his grandfather Edmund, and that's a blessing. Carolina's here standing in for her great uncle Morton, who I'm sorry to say has passed. And we'd have never met—" he paused for a moment, trying to drag the words up from the place in his chest that clutched at him in despair "—Avery and Debbie and Dinah without Darcy's help. And, you know, we almost pulled it off."

He felt the boys' falling expressions as if they physically pulled him down. Each frown was a lead weight pressing on his shoulders, each set of sad eyes a stab to his gut.

"As the new sign says, boys ranch has been here for seventy years, and it will go on for another seventy if I've anything to say about it."

Half-hearted cheers of "Sure will!" and other such encouragements did nothing to make the next words any easier.

"But it won't be here. Without Theodore Linley—my grandfather—the stipulations of Cyrus's will go unmet, and we'll have to move back to the old place and go on as we always have."

There. He'd said it. He'd admitted that his grandfather's continued disappearance was the failing link in this chain; he'd confessed that he hadn't found him. So far, the ground hadn't risen up and swallowed him whole, but he found himself wishing for it. Wishing he was anywhere but here, doing anything but this.

"You mean we really don't get to stay?" Diego asked.

Just when he thought it couldn't sting any worse. "No, son, we don't."

Desperation sent his eyes out over the gathering. He was beyond thankful when he saw that Avery had come back inside. Tears wet her cheeks. He locked his gaze onto her, needing to see her face while the world toppled around him. He'd remember last night's kisses as the only good thing to come out of this whole mess, and try to be thankful for that. He'd spent the day in hiding, sure he couldn't stomach the sight of her packing her things.

"I know that's a hard pill to swallow," he went on, working to keep his voice from wavering as Avery wiped fresh tears from her eyes. "But we'll get by. This isn't the first tough challenge you boys have had to face, and I know you'll find a way through. And we'll all help every single way we can." Right now, looking at the sea of disappointed faces, Gabe would put all of Five Rocks up on the block and buy the Triple C himself if it could be done.

But, of course, it couldn't. Mean ol' Cyrus had seen to that. *I hate you, old man.* The moment the words repeated in his mind, Gabe realized he couldn't rightly say if he was speaking to Cyrus or Theodore. *God have mercy on your mean old souls, the both of you.*

"I do have a bit of good news, though. The league has made it possible for all of you to go to the rodeo championships in Waco next weekend. All of you, up-front seats, as our gift to you."

There were some smiles, and genuine attempts at "isn't that nice?" from the adults, but it couldn't hope to put a dent in the sadness that filled the room. It was a fool's hope to think it ever would. How could one day—even one amazing day like they'd have at the championships—make up for losing the Triple C to a strip mall?

The room was excruciatingly quiet. Gabe had to fix this, to find some way out of this sad mess and save the evening. There had to be some words to let these kids know they were down but not out. Only he felt so down and out himself, everything he could think of felt hollow and pointless.

Gabe cleared his throat again, sending a silent "Help me!" plea to Heaven for something—anything—to redeem the moment.

"Can I say something?"

The whole room turned to Avery.

"I came here not sure I ever wanted anything to do with this place. I never knew much of Grandpa Cyrus, and what I've learned hasn't given me a lot of affection for the guy. I'm…well, I'm just plain sorry for what he's done to all of you. And if I had the power to change it, I'd do whatever it took. I just want you to know that."

Marlene, who was standing next to Avery and the girls, wiped a tear from her own face and reached out a hand to Avery's shoulder.

"But I want you to know something else, too," Avery went on. "Something Grandpa Cyrus did do, and something he can't take away from me no matter what scheme he pulls. And that's all of you."

She walked toward the stage as she continued talking. "I came here ready for everyone to be mean. To use me for whatever it was Grandpa Cyrus set me up to be. Only it didn't turn out that way. You all have treated me as nice as you ever could be. My girls and I both. And Gabe is right—the way you all pulled together for today is something special. Something even going back to the Silver Star won't take away from you."

I love that woman. He'd known it all along—since way back showing her the toolboxes—and he'd felt it in every corner of his soul last night. But right now, it was declaring itself to him in shouts that pounded inside his chest.

"But Gabe is wrong about something. If you knew how this man is beating himself up for failing you, for not finding a way to do what no one else in this room could do, either, your heart would break. I've never seen a man so relentlessly try for something. Not because he wanted it, but because you needed it."

She'd reached the stage now, and when Avery

reached for his hand, Gabe could not stop himself from taking it for all the world.

"And that's no failure," she said, smiling at him even as tears fell across her cheeks. "That's a man of honor, a man to be proud of." She hesitated just a moment, her face turning the most extraordinary shade of pink. "That's a man to love. Don't you dare let this man feel a failure for how hard he's tried on your behalf. Cyrus has taken a lot, but he doesn't get to take this from me. He brought me here, to you," she said, looking straight at Gabe, and he felt his heart gallop toward her. "And to all of you," she said to the crowd. "I've made a decision. I'd like to stay in Haven. I hope I can make my home here, if I can work it out, if you'll have me." She directed those last words at Gabe.

He wasn't a man for grand gestures. He wasn't much for speeches or public declarations. But there was only one response to a speech like that, and it didn't matter if there were one hundred or one thousand people watching. Gabe pulled Avery to him and kissed her for the true, extraordinary blessing she was. For taking the darkest moment of his life and filling it with light.

And love.

And tiny pinkness, for no sooner had he kissed her soundly than he felt the clamp of little-girl arms around his legs, squeezing him tight and yelling, "Hooray for Mr. Boots!"

She'd chosen Gabe, but then again, she hadn't. Avery stood there, watching Gabe tear his heart open in front of all those people who loved and respected him, and it was as if some irresistible force drew her to say what she did, despite all the obstacles still in her way. She had to walk toward him with her hand out. With her heart out, in defense and admiration and—yes—love for him.

Because she loved him, and she had to believe that love still conquered all.

It had begun to dawn on her late last night, while she sat in her bed trying to catalog all the reasons why it was safest to go back to Tennessee and put Haven behind her. Nothing Cyrus could leave her now would change anything—be it ten cabins, ten dollars or a fortune. Cyrus's manipulations were just an act taken by someone gone from her life. Standing outside just now, leaning against the barn, none of that mattered. Everything in the past didn't matter.

What mattered were the people in her life now, the man and the love this crazy situation had dropped in her lap. That was the true inheritance, the blessing that made everything else possible. The truth was that nothing of real value was waiting for her back in Tennessee; it all was here in Haven. In this loving community and in the love of a man who cared so much for her welfare that he was ready to deny himself that love. If God had brought her this far, couldn't she count on Him to tear down the obstacles that remained? Couldn't God give her the words to ask and receive Danny's consent to move to this place that now held the key to her happiness?

Given all that, was it really any surprise that she found herself kissing Gabe Everett in front of God and everybody in Haven, Texas? When the girls came up and wrapped her and Gabe in the wonderful circle of their arms, the last nigglings of doubt had vanished. Whatever lay in front of them because of Cyrus's crazy scheme, Haven would get through it. And she'd be there to help.

Avery didn't even hear the applause at first. She was lost in the wonder of Gabe's arms, in the exquisite perfectness of her love for him. They both realized the rather public nature of the display at the same time, pulling only a tiny bit from each other and laughing even as the girls giggled and jumped at their feet.

She could tell Gabe was grasping for what to say, but really, what was there to be said?

"I tried so hard not to fall for you," he finally whispered. "But it couldn't be helped."

Not the most romantic words ever to declare love, but to Avery, they were perfect, because they came from Gabe.

"I want to stay for you," she whispered back. "We all want to stay for you."

Evidently, the girls hadn't quite caught on to that until just now. "We can stay?" They began to chant, jumping up and down. "Mama says we're staying!"

"I sure hope so, sweetheart. I want to stay with Mr. Boots, don't you?"

Their smiles were all the answer she needed.

Suddenly, Jethro and Marlene were beside them, boasting mile-wide smiles themselves. Marlene grabbed the frame from the podium and handed it to Dinah, who rushed to hang it in its place on the stage vines. "We've been waiting for you two kids to figure this out," Jethro said with a tender chuckle. "You sure waited until the very last moment." He grinned at Avery. "Although I give ya points for drama. That was the sweetest speech I ever heard, young lady. Clearly, you don't take after the likes of your grandfather."

"I'm sorry about all that, really I am," Avery said. "I meant what I said. If there was any way I could change it, I'd do it. It wouldn't matter what it was, I'd do it."

"That's why I will," said a voice from the crowd, and the gathering parted to see Harley hobbling up toward the stage.

"Harley," Gabe said, helping the poor man step up onto the stage. "There isn't anything any of us can do."

Harold Haverman at least had the decency to look regretful when he agreed, "Not a thing. Cyrus's terms were explicit."

Harley coughed. "That's where you're wrong." He gestured toward the microphone, and Gabe stood back, but not before casting a curious glance toward Avery. She shrugged, having no more idea than Gabe did what Harley was up to.

"Hi, everyone. I'm Harley Jones, y'all know that."

As revelations go, that wasn't much of a start. A curious silence filled the room.

"Y'all been looking for Theodore Linley. And now all kinds of sadness is happening because he couldn't be found. And I was content to leave it that way, which is a stain on my part, because I've known all along where Theo was."

"Harley?" Gabe sputtered. Avery felt him stiffen beside her—and rightly so. To have gone through all he did when the solution was known?

Harley held up his hand to silence whatever Gabe was going to say. The old man gripped the podium, and Avery noticed his hands were shaking. What on earth was going on?

"Truth was, I thought it cost too much to tell you. Only today it's pretty clear it'll cost me much more to keep my mouth shut. The fact of the matter is that y'all have found Theodore Linley, and he's in this room. On account of…well, he's me."

The room buzzed with shock and disbelief. But as Avery stood looking at the two men, the resemblance jumped out at her. The jawline, the set of the eyebrows, the shape of their hands—he was kin to Gabe. And here she thought life in Haven couldn't get any more surprising.

"I ain't been a respectable man. I done things I can't be proud of, left when I shouldn't have and, well, I expect you know most of that on account of your lookin'. Always seemed to me that Gabe was better off without me. Only I couldn't stay totally away, so I signed on as a hand to my girl's new husband so's I could keep an eye on things—on my grandson—after she died."

He turned to look at Gabe. His eyes held such pain and regret that Avery nearly gasped. She felt Gabe tighten his hand on her and gave a silent prayer of thanks that she could stand beside him at a bombshell of a moment like this.

"It was a coward's way out, but then again, that's what I am. I figured Theo Linley was no good to anybody, especially you. And then all this business happened, and it got harder to keep my mouth shut. I'd have to fess up to all kinds of things, and I didn't think I could do it."

Gabe started to say something, but Harley—or was that now Theo?—held up his hand again.

"Let me finish, son. I got a lot of silence to make up for."

Son. The word hit Avery like a wall, and she could only imagine what it did to Gabe. It was a wonder the man was still upright.

"I made up my mind to stay away from today, to just let it all lie quiet and let Cyrus win whatever battle he'd claimed for himself." Theo coughed, hard this time, and shifted his weight. Gabe was not the only man baring his soul today at great cost, Avery thought.

"Only I couldn't. The ranch had been there for Gabe when I was too much of a mess to be there for him. I came here thinking I'd fess up, then I lost my nerve."

Avery remembered that "Harley" had left the party in the middle of it—she'd just figured he was tired and went home. She hadn't seen him come back in.

Theo's eyes returned to Gabe. "And I watched you come up here, strong and steady, and own up to bad news. Like a man ought to. Like the man I couldn't be."

The old man turned his eyes to Avery, and the lump in Avery's throat grew ten sizes. There was such a pained smile in the man's eyes she felt her own eyes well up with tears. "Then you came up here, sayin' what you said, and I realized I was even prouder than you were of Gabe. Of who he is, and the people who love him. Of you saying how you'd do whatever you could do to save the boys ranch, no matter what it cost. And here I was sitting on the only thing that could save it. So maybe, just this once, I figured I could step up and be half the man my grandson is today."

"You're Theo Linley." Gabe's voice was thick with emotion. Stunned, but with shock, not hate. "You're my grandfather."

"I am. And I'm beyond sorry for not telling you before this. I'll never be able to make that up to you, I know."

"By gum, Theo, it is you," Sam Teller shouted from his chair on the far side of the room. "I been trying to figure out why you looked familiar."

"You're my grandfather," Gabe repeated as if he couldn't get his mind around the idea. Of all the crazy things to happen since Avery came to Haven, this one topped the list.

"So now you found Theo Linley. You've saved the Triple C for the boys." Theo offered a small grin. "And got the girl, to boot. Not a bad day's work." He shrugged. "I'll go now and leave all y'all to celebratin'."

"You will not," Gabe said, walking toward the old man. After so many years of being denied their relationship, Avery wasn't sure what Gabe would say next.

Tears slid down her cheeks and Gabe grasped the old man's arm. "My grandfather isn't going to leave this party. Because I didn't save the ranch, Theo." Gabe choked on the name, and for the first time Avery heard him utter it with awe, not frustration. "You did." With that Gabe pulled Theo into a hug, sending the crowd bursting into applause.

"Hey," called Johnny, "that means we get to stay, right?"

"That it does," Harold Haverman announced.

"I can hardly believe it," Bea Brewster shouted as she hugged anyone within arm's reach. "Who'd have thought?"

Gabe was caught up in the moment with his grandfather, and Avery was glad for it, but then in a moment she found herself surrounded with well-wishers, too.

"I'm so happy for you," Josie said as she held baby Joy. "For both of you. For all five of you!"

It was true. Out of nowhere, out of strife and sorrow and scheming, God had crafted this amazing little family for her. It was a wonder. It was wonderful. Avery couldn't remember when she'd ever felt so happy.

"So this will be our new home, Mama?" Dinah asked.

"If Daddy says it's okay. Is that okay with you?" Avery brushed back her daughter's hair.

"Yup, yup, yup!" Dinah's head bobbed up and down gleefully with each word.

"You, too?" Avery asked Debbie.

"Twice as many *yup*s!" Debbie proclaimed. "Even my broke arm says *yup*."

"Now there's an endorsement if ever I heard one." Macy Swanson came up, arm in arm with Tanner Barstow. "Tanner's always said Gabe couldn't hold out his bachelor status too much longer with all this matchmaking going on."

"Oh," said Gabe as he came back to Avery's side, "they tried on us. Didn't realize it takes no arm twisting to coax me to Lila's for pie." He took Avery's hand. "Some things a man just has to figure out on his own."

Avery looked up at him and felt her heart glow. *I love him, Lord. And You knew that was coming all along. How can I doubt You'll work the rest out?*

Chapter Eighteen

Gabe smiled down at Avery. He could ponder the last thirty minutes for thirty years and still not grasp everything that had happened. Today was supposed to be one of the worst days of his life, and wasn't it just like God to turn the whole thing on its ear in ways he never imagined?

A thought struck him. "Do you think Cyrus knew what he was really doing?"

Harold Haverman gave a doubtful smirk. "Let's just say I'm of a mind that what Cyrus meant for orneriness, God meant for good."

Gabe looked at Harley... *Theo*—it'd take a while before that adjustment sunk in. His grandfather was talking in animated tones with Samuel Teller and Edmund Grayson. His *grandfather*. Right under his nose all these years. Suddenly, the powerful connection he'd always felt with Harley Jones made sense. Theo may have believed he could never be there for Gabe, but Harley had been there. In a hundred ways over the years. There was so much surprise and astonishment in his heart—especially now with Avery—that there wasn't any room for judgment or resentment. Only love, and loads of it.

Gabe pulled Avery to his side. "I love you," he whispered into her ear despite the many people surrounding them. "Have I said that yet?"

She smiled up at him with glistening, tear-filled eyes. "Not in words."

"I love you," he repeated, finding a startling delight in uttering them. "In words, this time."

"And swings, and tea parties, and doctor visits, and tumble-down cabins...and a few rather persuasive kisses." Her cheeks turned the most distracting shade of pink. "But the words are nice, too."

"Speaking of tumble-down cabins," Haverman said. Gabe tried not to begrudge the attorney for horning in on his happy moment. "Miss Avery, I believe we have some unfinished business."

"The rest of Cyrus's bequest," Gabe added. In all of the drama, he'd half forgotten that the other portion of Cyrus's will for Avery would be revealed if she stayed until today.

Harold produced an envelope from his jacket pocket. "I've no idea what's in here, miss. Don't think I've been holding out on you." He handed the envelope to Avery, who took it with an expression that seemed half curiosity, half apprehension. Gabe didn't blame her one bit. Based on Cyrus, and today, Gabe was ready to think just about anything could happen.

Avery opened the envelope and unfolded the single sheet of paper. Gabe longed to read over her shoulder, but stood silently in front of her. After a moment, however, neither man could show much more patience, and Harold said, "Well?"

"He's made me beneficiary of a three-hundred-thousand-dollar life insurance policy in addition to the cabin. 'Enough to make a home and a life in Haven if you choose,' he says." She also shook the envelope to let a key slide out. "And this is to a safe-deposit box that's filled with family photos and my grandmother's jewelry."

She looked up at Gabe, blinking away tears. "I didn't know any of that existed. I thought it all was lost. Daddy never talked about any of it." She turned the key over in her palm. "When Rhetta gave me that one photo, it made me so lonesome for more—for any bits of my family. And now I have a whole bunch of them."

"And a nice little sum to set you up comfortably," Harold added. "I know he could be a stubborn old goat, but I like to think Cyrus wanted to do good by you in the end." Harold stared out at the party, still in full swing. "Look at them. Theodore, Samuel, Edmund, the boys in their new home, you two—could you ever think Cyrus could do so much good while putting us through so much trouble?"

Gabe put his arm around Avery. "He always did have a talent for stirring things up."

"I suppose he's having a good laugh right about now," Avery said. Gabe reveled in the way her arm slipped about his waist. She felt so perfect settled under his arm—it made him wonder how he hadn't noticed how empty his arms were before they held this marvelous woman.

"I can't believe I'm saying this, but thank God for Cyrus Culpepper." True enough, Gabe did feel an honest sense of gratitude to God for what Cyrus's crazy scheme had brought him. One look into Avery's eyes told him she felt the same way.

Suddenly, a burst of cheers went up in the far corner of the room. Harold, Avery and Gabe all looked at each other. "What now?" Harold asked, echoing what Gabe was thinking.

Seconds later Marlene came up with a huge smile. "Well, that molasses of a man finally did what he oughta," she declared.

"Meaning?" Gabe asked.

"Pastor Andrew finally found his nerve and popped the question to Katie Ellis. Just now in front of God and everybody."

Avery nodded her head toward the hugs and laughter bursting out of that corner of the room. "And she said yes?"

Marlene chuckled. "Honey, I don't even think she let him finish the question."

Gabe watched as several men clasped the pastor on the back. "Some days I think that reverend was the last person in town to realize how sweet Katie was on him."

Marlene gave Gabe a look. "Some men just take their time wising up to things, don't they?"

A week later, Avery sat nestled against Gabe on the porch staring up at the brilliant collection of Texas spring stars. This had become their favorite time of day, when the house was quiet and the girls were tucked away in bed. "Well, that's the last call. I've thanked them all for praying while I talked to Danny."

Gabe exhaled in relief. "With that many prayer

warriors lined up, he didn't stand any hope of saying no to your request."

"It didn't take much convincing, actually. When I told him how happy I'd become here, how the girls loved it, he said yes. Almost right away. I treated him like Cyrus, Gabe. I turned him into some kind of monster based on how abandoned I felt. But he isn't. He's far from perfect, but he wants what's best for the girls." She looked at Gabe. "And that's you."

His eyes glowed. "I love those girls. I love their mama even more." He kissed her again, long and slow and full of wonder. The last of the obstacles had been removed, and the world was settling down into a perfect future for her and the girls.

"I've been thinking about what to do with the money Grandpa Cyrus left me."

Gabe's arm tightened around her. "Have you, now?"

"Of course, I'll need some of it to restart my decorating business down here. But I've been thinking about how different my life would have been if I'd have had a place like the ranch. So many boys' lives have been changed. Why not girls' lives? The cabin isn't big enough, but the land around it is. Maybe there's just enough to start renovating and expanding that old place."

Gabe's gaze fell out over the land in the direction of the boys ranch. "I think it's a great idea. I expect the league would donate toward the cause in a heartbeat." He planted a tender kiss on her forehead. "The president is rather fond of you, you know."

"Well, yes, there's that. And I rather like the idea of Cyrus doing even more good than he planned."

He carefully took both her hands in his as he slowly asked, "But if you give away the property for a girls ranch, where will you live?"

She turned to look at him. She'd been trying to find a way to say this for a week now, but couldn't work out how or when. "There's only one place in Haven I want to call home." She took a deep breath. "So you'd better hurry up, cowboy."

Gabe's eyes took on a playful gleam. He had clearly caught her meaning, but pasted a puzzled look on his face and asked, "Hurry up and what?"

She sat up and yanked on the hands he was holding. "You molasses of a man. Am I gonna have to call over a crowd of mystery matchmakers from the ranch to explain it for you?"

"Well, I don't know. What do I need with a bunch of meddling boys when I've got this?" With that, Avery watched Gabe slip one of his hands from hers and reach down under the wicker couch. His hand came back up with a small black box.

Avery's heart bubbled up like a fountain at the sight of the glistening ring inside. It sparkled like the starlight she loved so much in the sky above Five Rocks.

Gabe's eyes grew intense. "I know it's quick, but I'm done waiting. I'd have done it even sooner but I knew you needed word from Danny. And now we've got that, and I don't ever want you to leave Five Rocks. Not for a day. So I figured I better make an honest woman out of you fast as I can."

"Gabe." It felt so splendid to sigh his name. Yes, it was quick, but even the girls had sensed how things had settled down in perfect places. Gabe was an honorable man. If they waited, he would insist they move off Five Rocks, and she knew what he knew: no one wanted that. If putting plans in place to become a family—the family they had in many ways already become—meant moving quickly, then Avery felt they couldn't move quickly enough. The girls deserved to stay where they were for the same reason she did: they loved it here.

All of this was rushing through her heart so fast that Avery didn't realize Gabe was staring at her. "Speaking of slow as molasses…" he said, raising one playful eyebrow.

She'd already said yes so many times in her heart it had escaped her she hadn't voiced the words. "It's yes! It was yes before you ever asked." She kissed him soundly, just to underscore her point.

When they pulled apart, breathless with happiness, Avery thought of something. "How shall we tell the girls?"

Gabe actually blushed a bit—something so endearing Avery thought her heart might actually burst. "Well," he said, reaching into his shirt pocket, "I've been thinking on that." He produced a little silk bag. "I figure I ought to ask them, too. And when I saw these in town, I knew just how."

He opened Avery's hand and spilled the contents of the little bag into her palm. Two silver rings tumbled out with a jingle—tiny but real silver and inlaid with sparkly mother-of-pearl.

In the shape of cowboy boots. "How else would Mr. Boots ask for their hand…hands?"

"Oh, Gabe, they'll just die of happiness." She slid her arms around his neck. "I think I already have. If

I didn't want you all to myself, I might just go and wake them up right now."

Gabe's eyes burned with the same glow that filled her heart. "It can wait. Right now, I just want to kiss my wife. My future wife." And he did.

"How does tomorrow sound?" he asked, his voice so breathless she tingled all the way to the tips of her toes.

"Too soon," she laughed into his chest.

"Can't blame a man for trying."

Avery held up her hand, watching the diamond sparkle in the moonlight. "Now that I think about it, I could be persuaded to consider next week."

He grinned. "I've been told I'm very persuasive."

"I've been thanking God twelve times a day you persuaded me to bring the girls out to Five Rocks. For all of it. I know all this craziness seemed chaotic and unfair along the way, but I can see it all leading to this now. To us, together. And I'm glad. I never thought I'd say it, but I'm glad."

Gabe pulled her back against his chest and they settled in together to stare up at the brilliant sky of stars. "I believe I am the happiest man in Haven, Texas. Maybe the whole world." She felt his chin settle against the top of her head. "It is an amazing thing, my loving you. I hope it never stops startling me every time I think it."

"Why Gabriel Everett, what a downright romantic thing to say."

She could hear the smile in his tone. "A tidal wave of tiny pinkness will do that to a man."

* * * * *

A new LONE STAR COWBOY LEAGUE
*miniseries from Love Inspired Historical
is coming in April 2017!*

Don't miss
LONE STAR COWBOY LEAGUE:
MULTIPLE BLESSINGS.
*Be sure to turn the page for a special excerpt
from the first book,*
THE RANCHER'S SURPRISE TRIPLETS
by Linda Ford

If you liked this
LONE STAR COWBOY LEAGUE:
BOYS RANCH *novel,
make sure you read the entire miniseries:*

Book #1: THE RANCHER'S TEXAS MATCH
by Brenda Minton
Book #2: THE RANGER'S TEXAS PROPOSAL
by Jessica Keller
Book #3: THE NANNY'S TEXAS CHRISTMAS
by Lee Tobin McClain
Book #4: THE COWBOY'S TEXAS FAMILY
by Margaret Daley
Book #5: THE DOCTOR'S TEXAS BABY
by Deb Kastner
Book #6: THE RANCHER'S TEXAS TWINS
by Allie Pleiter

Dear Reader,

Just when we think we've got our plans worked out, God goes ahead and throws a huge wrench into them. That's always for the best, but we rarely see it that way at the time. Gabe thinks he is incapable of the kind of love Avery and her girls need, but the truth is he is more than capable when he breaks the shackles of his past. Avery thinks her heart can't trust the speed at which it awakens to Gabe, but it's God's perfect timing in a place she'd never expect.

I hope this story leads you to look for God's gifts in unexpected places. I'd love to hear from you! You can reach me on my website *alliepleiter.com*, via email at *allie@alliepleiter.com* or good old-fashioned paper mail at P.O. Box 7026, Villa Park, IL 60181. You can also find me on Twitter @alliepleiter or on my Facebook Author Page. Drop me a line!

COMING NEXT MONTH FROM
Love Inspired®

Available March 21, 2017

HER SECRET AMISH CHILD
Pinecraft Homecomings • by Cheryl Williford

Returning to her Amish community, Lizbeth Mullet comes face-to-face with her teenage crush, Fredrik Lapp. As he builds a bond with her son and she falls for him all over again, will revealing the secret she holds turn out to be their undoing—or the key to their happily-ever-after?

THE COWBOY'S EASTER FAMILY WISH
Wranglers Ranch • by Lois Richer

Widowed single mom Maddie McGregor moved to Tucson, Arizona, for a fresh start with her son. She never expected Noah's healing would be helped along by the former youth minister working at Wranglers Ranch—or that Jesse Parker could also be her hope for a second chance at forever.

EASTER IN DRY CREEK
Dry Creek • by Janet Tronstad

Clay West is back in Dry Creek, Montana, to prove he's innocent of the crime he was convicted for. But when he reconnects with old friend Allie Nelson, his biggest challenge will be showing her not only that he's a good man—but that he's the perfect man for *her*.

WINNING OVER THE COWBOY
Texas Cowboys • by Shannon Taylor Vannatter

When Landry Malone arrives in Bandera, Texas, to claim her inheritance of half a dude ranch, co-owner Chase Donovan plans to run her out and keep his family legacy. Landry is just as determined to show the cowboy she's up for the challenge of running the place—and winning his heart.

WILDFIRE SWEETHEARTS
Men of Wildfire • by Leigh Bale

As a hotshot crew member, Tessa Carpenter is always ready to fight wildfire. Yet nothing could've prepared her for having her ex-fiancé as her boss. Sean Nash's guilt over Tessa's brother's death caused him to end their engagement. Now he's bent on getting back the love of his life.

THEIR SECOND CHANCE LOVE
Texas Sweethearts • by Kat Brookes

Hope Dillan is back in Texas to help her ailing father recover. Making sure his nursery business stays afloat will mean working with Logan Cooper—the sweetheart she's never forgotten. To embrace a future together, can she finally reveal the secret that tore them apart?

LICNM0317

Get 2 Free Books,

Plus 2 Free Gifts—

just for trying the Reader Service!

SPECIAL EXCERPT FROM

Love Inspired **HISTORICAL**

*When local rancher Bo Stillwater finds abandoned triplet
babies at the county fair, the first person he turns to is
doctor's daughter Louisa Clark. But as they open their
hearts to the children, they might discover unexpectedly
tender feelings for one another taking root.*

Read on for a sneak preview of
THE RANCHER'S SURPRISE TRIPLETS,
the touching beginning of the series
**LONE STAR COWBOY LEAGUE:
MULTIPLE BLESSINGS.**

"Doc? I need to see the doctor."

Father had been called away. Whatever the need, she would
have to take care of it. She opened the door and stared at Bo in
surprise until crying drew her attention to the cart beside him.

"Babies? What are you doing with babies?" All three crying
and looking purely miserable.

"I think they're sick. They need to see the doctor."

"Bring them in. Father is away but I'll look at them."

"They need a doctor." He leaned to one side to glance into
the house as if to make sure she wasn't hiding her father. "When
will he be back?"

"I'll look at them," she repeated. "I've been my father's
assistant for years. I'm perfectly capable of checking a baby.
Bring them in." She threw back the door so he could push the
cart inside. She bent over to look more closely at the babies.
"We don't see triplets often." She read their names on their
shirts. "Hello, Jasper, Eli and Theo."

They were fevered and fussy. Theo reached his arms toward
her. She lifted him and cradled him to her shoulder. "There,

there, little man. We'll fix you up in no time."

Jasper, seeing his brother getting comfort, reached out his arms, too.

Louisa grabbed a kitchen chair and sat, putting Theo on one knee and lifting Jasper to the other. The babies were an armload. At first glance they appeared to be in good health. But they were fevered. She needed to speak to the mother about their age and how long they'd been sick.

Eli's wails increased at being left alone.

"Can you pick him up?" she asked Bo, hiding a smile at his hesitation. Had he never held a baby? At first he seemed uncertain what to do, but Eli knew and leaned his head against Bo's chest. Bo relaxed and held the baby comfortably enough. Louisa grinned openly as the baby's cries softened. "He's glad for someone to hold him. Where are the parents?"

"Well, that's the thing. I don't know."

"You don't know where the parents are?"

He shook his head. "I don't even know *who* they are."

"Then why do you have the babies?"

For an answer, he handed her a note and she read it. "They're abandoned?" She pulled each baby close as shock shuddered through her. He explained how he'd found them in the pie tent.

"I must find their mother before she disappears." Bo looked at Louisa, his eyes wide with appeal, the silvery color darkened with concern for these little ones. "I need to go but how are you going to manage?"

She wondered the same thing. But she would not let him think she couldn't do it. "I'll be okay. Put Eli down. I'll take care of them."

Don't miss
THE RANCHER'S SURPRISE TRIPLETS *by Linda Ford,*
available April 2017 wherever
Love Inspired® Historical books and ebooks are sold.

www.LoveInspired.com

SPECIAL EXCERPT FROM

*Returning to her Amish community, Lizbeth Mullet comes
face-to-face with her teenage crush, Fredrik Lapp. As he
builds a bond with her son and she falls for him all over
again, will revealing the secret she holds turn out to be their
undoing—or the key to their happily-ever-after?*

Read on for a sneak preview of
HER SECRET AMISH CHILD by **Cheryl Williford**,
available April 2017 from Love Inspired!

"Lie still. You may have broken something," Lizbeth
instructed.

His hand moved and then his arm. Blue eyes—so like
her son's—opened to slits. He blinked at her. A shaggy brow
arched in question. Full, well-shaped lips moved, but no
words came out.

She leaned back in surprise. The man on the ground was
Fredrik Lapp, her brother's childhood friend. The last man in
Pinecraft she wanted to see. "Are you all right?" she asked,
bending close.

His coloring looked normal enough, but she knew nothing
about broken bones or head trauma. She looked down the
length of his body. His clothes were dirty but seemed intact.

The last time she'd seen him, she'd been a skinny girl of
nineteen, and he'd been a wiry young man of twenty-three.
Now he was a fully matured man. One who could rip her life
apart if he learned about the secret she'd kept all these years.

He coughed several times and scowled as he drew in a

LIEXP0317

deep breath.

"Is the *kinner* all right?" Fredrik's voice sounded deeper and raspier than it had years ago. With a grunt, he braced himself with his arms and struggled into a sitting position.

Lizbeth glanced Benuel's way. He was looking at them, his young face pinched with concern. Her heart ached for the intense, worried child.

"*Ya*, he's fine," she assured Fredrik and tried to hold him down as he started to move about. "Please don't get up. Let me get some help first. You might have really hurt yourself."

He ignored her direction and rose to his feet, dusting off the long legs of his dark trousers. "I got the wind knocked out of me, that's all."

He peered at his bleeding arm, shrugged his broad shoulders and rotated his neck as she'd seen him do a hundred times as a boy.

"That was a foolish thing you did," he muttered, his brow arched.

"What was?" she asked, mesmerized by the way his muscles bulged along his freckled arm. It had to be wonderful to be strong and afraid of nothing.

He gestured toward the boy. "Letting your *soh* run wild like that? He could have been killed. Why didn't you hold his hand while you crossed the road?"

Don't miss
HER SECRET AMISH CHILD by Cheryl Williford,
available April 2017 wherever
Love Inspired® books and ebooks are sold.

www.LoveInspired.com

Turn your love of reading into
rewards you'll love with

Harlequin My Rewards

**Join for FREE today at
www.HarlequinMyRewards.com**

Earn **FREE BOOKS** of your choice.

Experience **EXCLUSIVE OFFERS** and contests.

Enjoy **BOOK RECOMMENDATIONS**
selected just for you.

PLUS! Sign up now
and get **500** points
right away!

Earn
FREE
REWARDS
HarlequinMyRewards.com
Join
Today!